DEADLY FROST

KARI LEE HARMON

OLIVER HEBER BOOKS

PRAISE FOR THE COLDWATER COVE SERIES

"This story does not end with the killer you are expecting. It is a romantic suspense that is heavy on the suspense. Stacy is home to settle her dad's affairs and finally figure out who killed her mom. Trent is on a hunt for redemption of his father's good name with the FBI to prove there is a killer loose in the town. The author is able to keep the reader guessing until the killer is revealed by pulling threads and throwing misdirections. This is very well done and makes for an interesting plot and a great story."--***Top Amazon Reviewer***

"Dark Seas by Kari Lee Harmon is a novel set in the harbor town of Coldwater Cove, Maine. Harmon weaves together 2 cases with style and artistry. The plot line moves swiftly and the characters are relatable. It's a murder mystery that will keep you on your toes. Billed as book 1 of Coldwater Cove, I look forward to more in the series."--***Top Amazon Reviewer***

"This excellent romantic suspense kept me turning the pages. I enjoyed it and would recommend it to those who like stories with romance, mystery, and suspense. I look forward to reading what comes next in this series."--*Top Amazon Reviewer*

"If you enjoy a book with twists and turns, is suspenseful, has murder and mystery along with romance, this book is for you. I enjoyed the book from the first chapter until the last. I would recommend this book to anyone who enjoys action, adventure, strong women, dependability and loyalty, family, action, suspense, mystery, solving murder and, of course, romance. This is an exciting romance suspense book."--*Top Amazon Reviewer*

"This is my first book by Kari and let me tell you it will not be the last!!! Wow, so much intrigue, so many secrets. I usually read historical romance, or regency. This book will grab you with the first page. There are a lot of characters, and each has his or her own secrets and past. This book has so much mystery and suspense you just can't put it down. Just when you think you have figured it all out, wham the story takes a hard right and you're wrong!! Kari will have you guessing till the end. There is romance too but woven into the story. This is not a romance story; it is a mystery with lots of intrigue, twists, and turns. I can't wait to see what book two will be!! Rush to get your copy, but don't plan on getting anything else done until you finish it...enjoy."--*Top Amazon Reviewer*

"Harmon is a masterful storyteller who weaves together a fascinating tale of betrayal, redemption and love. The characters will captivate you. It is a phenomenal addition to the series."--*Top Amazon Reviewer*

"There are some wonderful characters and intense scenes. Emma and Gunner grow close and find a bond and lasting love as they solve the crime."— *Top Amazon Reviewer*

I enjoyed this excellent story and would recommend it to those who like stories with romance, mystery, and suspense. This tale is sure to keep you on the edge of your seat."-- *Top Amazon Reviewer*

Harmon's second book in her Coldwater Cove romantic suspense series is as interesting and fast-paced as the first one. It definitely kept me on my toes with its many twists and turns, danger, and possible suspects. It's a gripping tale that had me swiping pages as fast as I could, just to read what happens next. Emma had a few "what were you thinking" moments, and Gunner could have not let his past betrayal affect his present...but I loved the two of them together. Their chemistry and the heat from their smexytimes was off the charts. And Emma's Dream Team of JoJo and Harvey had me completely entertained. Then came the ending and I was blown away by who the mastermind was. An entertaining book from the first page until the last. I highly recommend this enthralling romantic suspense and look forward to the next book in the series. Each book stands alone, but I think you should read them all for maximum enjoyment."-- *Top Amazon Reviewer*

This is a new to me author and I LOVED the story. Loaded with angst and suspense, well developed characters and a non-stop story line, this book was a winner from the first to the last. Hard to put down. I started the series here and it does work as a standalone but it was good enough that I'll go pick up the previous book which I understand takes place in the same town."-- *Top Amazon Reviewer*

Dear DIL,
I'm dedicating this book to you, my very creative and talented daughter-in-law, Sam Wilks. Thank you for your brilliant inspiration and brainstorming session. I couldn't have pulled this one off without you.
Until next time...
With love,
MIL

"It's so nice to meet you, Dr. Sweeney." Sparrow James held out her hand to her new boss, Wildlife Director Dr. Victoria Sweeney.

The Maine Department of Agriculture, Conservation, and Forestry of State Parks and Public Lands had several separate offices located throughout the state. Coldwater Cove was located so far north that when they found they needed a new satellite office, they joined forces with the other departments to share the same building located on the edge of town near the woods.

Dr. Sweeney was the person who doled out the field assignments to the wildlife biologists regarding conservation in the northern coastal region. This arrangement allowed them to work closely with the agriculture and forestry departments.

"Please, call me Victoria." The tall woman sporting silver hair pulled high in a ponytail, faded blue eyes, no makeup, blue jeans, and a sweatshirt thrust out her hand and shook Sparrow's hard. "We aren't so formal around here. No suits and ties for us, either."

"Good to know." Sparrow smiled wide, thankful she could ditch the blazer and dress pants. Not that she didn't like to dress up, but she preferred field work over sitting at a desk any day.

"Northern Maine's climate can be brutal when she wants to be, so we care more about common sense and appropriate attire than looking snazzy. We do have various items with our logo on it like hats, vests, coats, and badges, but we don't wear uniforms like the Rangers do. It's up to you what you wear, so long as you're sporting our logo somewhere, so folks know who you are."

Back in Washington, Sparrow had worked for a private lab, where the dress code and overall culture had been a lot stricter and less friendly. I looked like working at the Maine organization would be a refreshing change. She hoped it stayed that way.

All wildlife biologists wanted the same things: to protect and preserve wild animals and their ecosystems, but sometimes state and government agencies could butt heads with private labs and nonprofit organizations. She'd experienced that firsthand in the past and sure hoped it wouldn't be the case this time around.

"This here's Senior Wildlife Biologist Christopher Higgins." Victoria's words snapped Sparrow back to attention. She had a bad habit of daydreaming at the worst moments, and it had cost her dearly in the past.

"*Dr.* Higgins." The completely bald short man, with small spectacles that magnified his intelligent light brown eyes, pushed his glasses up his nose.

Victoria rolled her eyes and barked out a laugh. "Most of us are PhD's or have a master's degree, *Chris*. No need to get all fancy with each other. We'll save our titles for outsiders. Around here, some of us just have more years' experience, is all."

His face flushed red.

"It's nice to meet you, Dr. Higgins." Sparrow smiled gently at him and held out her hand, waiting patiently.

"Chris is fine." He cleared his throat then shook her hand limply.

"Now that that's settled, Chris here will be your direct contact during your field work. We have offices up and down both coasts, and Chris has worked in several. We're lucky to have him at our office here in Coldwater Cove. He will determine which methods to use for evaluating, collecting, and testing samples from the ecosystem you're assigned to."

"I look forward to working with someone of your experience," Sparrow said to Chris. He nodded once, but she noticed his chest puff up ever so slightly, and she bit back a smile.

Victoria motioned a curvy woman with a long thick blue braid forward. "Next up is Wildlife Assistant Lily Brown. She will be at your disposal for assistance with anything you might need."

Lily had emerald-green eyes that sparkled with excitement and dimples when she smiled. She held out her hand, her smile widening. "I have been so looking forward to meeting you, Sparrow. I just love field work."

Sparrow shook the bubbly woman's hand. "Likewise. I have to say I'm eager to get started. I think we'll make a great team."

"I have one team that's been working on a field project regarding the endangered New England cottontail in the meadows all summer, as well as another team who has been researching the little brown bats in caves in the mountains," Victoria stated. "Your specialty is birds. That's why I hired you. Lily is into birds as well."

"Fantastic." Sparrow nodded. Her mother had loved birds, this her name, and Sparrow had inherited the same trait. That was what drew her to the field in the first place.

"As you know, birding in Maine is a year-round activity. Many species migrate here in the spring, attracting birdwatchers from all over. June and July are filled with breeding activity. Then late August brings on the fall migration. After the woods go quiet in late summer, the birdwatchers head to the coast." Victoria pointed to a large map of Maine hanging on the wall.

Sparrow walked over and joined her, studying the map as Victoria continued.

"Our forest songbirds began flocking in August, with their fall migration building and peaking in September. Many species head to the ends of peninsulas and offshore islands. I've had a team inland capturing, collaring, and tracking members of various species all summer before their migration. Now that it's fall, it only made sense to send that team to the coast. The fall migration will continue well through October and into November for the waterfowl that will take up residence and stay along the coast through the winter."

"Where does that leave my team?"

"As you know land birds can be scarce during the coldest winter months, but that doesn't mean they aren't there. Now that we're well into fall, we need to be prepared and make sure their ecosystem is intact. I would like your team to survey and restore any damages inland to the habitat as well as study any Rough-legged Hawks, Snowy Owls, Northern Shrikes, Bohemian Waxwings, or Northern Finches you might see. Does that sound like something you can handle?" Victoria arched a thin gray brow at her.

"Give me some time to do some preparation, and I'm on it." Sparrow nodded once, already mentally making plans.

"I knew I liked you." Victoria grinned, then looked

around the room and clapped her hands. "Okay, everyone, daylight's a-wasting. You all have your assignments, and I'm here if you need anything."

Sparrow waited for everyone to leave before approaching her boss. "Thank you, Victoria. I appreciate you giving me the opportunity to prove myself."

Victoria stared at Sparrow for a long moment. "We've all been through tough times, Sparrow, but you shouldn't let that ruin the rest of your life." Sparrow's troubled past had been disclosed during the interview process, so Victoria knew all about her. "You're a gifted biologist, and it would have been a shame to let you waste that talent when it's so needed around these parts."

"Thank you. That means a lot."

Victoria tilted her head. "Don't thank me. Prove me right."

"I will."

"Okay, then. Forest Ranger Greyson Adler is in the office just down the hall. Anything you need to get started, I'm sure he'll be happy to help."

"Thanks again." Sparrow smiled genuinely as renewed excitement, which she hadn't felt in far too long for the work she did, fueled her being and fed her soul. She headed down the hall, eager to get started on a future that was trouble-free.

* * *

"DAMN IT." Greyson Adler pounded his fist on his desk as he read the latest report to come in. The poachers were at it again.

Wildlife crime was a big business across the country. Dangerous international networks trafficked wildlife and animal parts from all sorts of areas much like illegal drugs, weapons, and humans were. The illegal wildlife trade made billions of dollars.

In northern Maine, it was illegal to possess or sell wild birds, bears, deer, moose, and wild turkeys.. Countless other species were similarly exploited, from marine turtles to timber trees, especially in Maine.

Wild plants and animals from tens of thousands of species were caught or harvested legally and then sold legitimately. Hunting was legal during certain times if you had a license, and licensed hunters could get a special permit for moose, but there were laws that had to be followed.

The problem occurred when wildlife trade happened illegally. It was unsustainable—directly threatening the survival of many species in the wild. Stamping out wildlife crime was a top priority for the game wardens in the area.

Since that department was small, forest rangers like Greyson helped out whenever they could. Poaching was the biggest threat to the future of many of Maine's most endangered species, second only to the destruction of a species' habitat.

Lately, poaching in the northern Maine woods was at its highest.

Coldwater Cove was close to the vast Canadian border, with Nova Scotia right across the way. The waters were deep by the rough untamed shores, making it easy to smuggle goods either across the border or onto a ship without ever having to go through customs.

His cellphone rang, and he answered. "Ranger Adler here."

"Greyson, it's Wanda. Did you read the report yet?"

Wanda Thorndike was the Department of Forestry Manager he reported to. She was an impressive woman, six-feet tall with a strong, athletic frame, short espresso hair, honey-colored eyes, and milk chocolate skin. He'd worked for a lot of people, but she was by far the best boss he'd ever had. She truly cared about the environment.

He sighed and rubbed his eyes, trying to get rid of the headache building behind them. It was going to be another long day. "Just now," he responded. "We really need more game wardens, boss. Ever since Cole left, we can't keep up."

Cole Wilcox had been the game warden Greyson had worked closely with for years. He'd moved down south to take care of his elderly parents, and the entire department of forestry and agriculture had been short-staffed ever since.

"I hear you." Wanda's voice was filled with the same frustration Greyson felt. "His department has all their other wardens out in the field. They're working on re-placing Wilcox, but in the meantime, we'll have to pick up the slack. Finding another game warden who's both qualified and willing to live in such a harsh climate isn't easy."

"Understood. What do you want me to do? The woods are so vast, it's hard to monitor everywhere effi-ciently, especially since my assistant is on vacation."

Willy Tucker had been Greyson's assistant forest ranger for going on two years, but the kid was always taking time off or calling in sick. It was hard to do Greyson's job well or safely without a good assistant.

"For starters, set up more security cameras, work with the wildlife biologists on getting reports from the species they've caught and collared to see if any are missing, make more frequent patrols of the area, and have everyone keep their eyes and ears open. It's all we can do until more help is hired or returns from the field."

"Done."

"If it comes to it, we can always involve Sheriff West

and Chief Masters. You know they would be happy to help."

"After the damage from the winter nor'easter and the string of murders this past spring, they've barely had the summer to recover. I'm hoping this is something we can take care of ourselves."

"I have Brook on assignment along the coast with her assistant, and you inland, plus a few other teams scattered about, so give a shout if you need help. I don't mind getting back in the field myself if you need me."

"Roger that. In the meantime, I'll keep you posted."

"Be careful out there, Greyson. I don't have to tell you how much money is involved in illegal wildlife trading. These people are ruthless professionals."

"Will do." Greyson hung up and started gathering his things to leave when a knock sounded on his office door. "Come in," he beckoned, never expecting to get sucker-punched in the gut by the vision that walked into his life.

"Forest Ranger Greyson Adler?" she asked with a voice that sounded sweet and lyrical like a songbird.

He nodded slowly, just staring at her, then cleared his throat. "You can call me Greyson. And you are?"

"Wildlife Biologist Sparrow James, and you can call me Sparrow." Her smile was engaging, and her eyes sparkled with enthusiasm as she held out her hand.

He'd never seen anyone who looked like her before. Certainly not anyone from around these parts, and he'd been born and raised in Coldwater Cove. Sparrow James lived up to her name with her songbird voice and her colorful appearance.

She was a petite thing with a small frame, silky straight burgundy hair that fell all one length in a short bob just above her shoulders, and eyes that mesmerized him. They were such a pale gray they almost looked clear and were surrounded by the longest, thickest black eyelashes he had ever seen.

What the hell was wrong with him?

Greyson frowned, his mind buzzing. He'd never had this reaction to any woman before. She arched a brow, with her hand still outstretched, and he just stared at her for a moment before shaking himself out of his stupor.

"Sorry." He wrapped her small hand in his much bigger one and shook. "I kind of got lost in my thoughts."

She laughed, and his heart fluttered. "That's funny. I do the same thing way too often, so I get it. No worries."

He let go of her hand after realizing he'd held it a little too long. "It's very nice to meet you, Sparrow. What can I help you with today?"

"Well, I'm new to town. In fact, today is my first day on the job. I'm starting to prep a field work assignment inland, so I have some questions I wanted to ask you if you have some time."

"First off, welcome to town. Where are you staying?"

"Coldwater Commons. I figured a hotel would be good to start with because I could be in the field for weeks. I'll find a more permanent place to live once I'm back."

"Well, we have Johnson Family Finds. There are two brothers and one sister in the realtor team, and they're second to none. I'm sure they can help when you're ready."

"That would be wonderful. Thanks for the tip. So, about those questions."

"You don't waste any time getting started, do you? Have you even unpacked yet or taken a tour of The Cove?"

She blushed and bit her full bottom lip, nearly un-doing him. "I did unpack…sort of. I'm just so excited to get started." Her smile dimmed slightly. "I need a fresh start."

He could relate.

His mother, Carolyn, went missing five years ago, and his father, Mason, had been under suspicion for her disappearance. Her body was never found, but the suspicious cloud hanging over his father had ruined him until he could no longer cope and just up and left town.

Greyson had spent the past five years alone, looking for his mother and trying to reach his father, to no avail. He spent the rest of his time doing forest ranger work. He had no social life outside of that, other than the occasional one-night stand with tourists. He'd never given much thought to finding a partner of his own and settling down until this very moment.

Sparrow James was special.

"I know all about needing a fresh start. My life has been a little stagnant as well." He stood up, and she blinked. "Have you been to The Claw yet?"

She eyed him warily for a moment as she shook her head.

He looked at his watch. "How about lunch?"

"Oh…I…um."

"A girl's gotta eat, right?"

"I suppose so." She tucked her hair behind her ears.

Her eyes were troubled. It was clear she'd been through something. "It's just lunch, Sparrow. And while we're there, I can answer your questions. Sound good?"

She nodded.

"Great. It's a date." He grabbed his coat.

Her eyes widened and she didn't speak, but she grabbed her backpack and followed him out the door. He didn't want to scare her away like a frightened little bird, but he'd been dead inside since his mother disappeared and father left. Sparrow James was the first person to stir something inside of him in years. She'd said yes to lunch.

It wasn't much, but it was a start...and he was a patient man.

2

Sparrow climbed out of Greyson's jeep in the parking lot of the marina, wandering forward as she took in the view.

Coldwater Cove was a small, picturesque seaside fishing village. The harbor was filled with fishing boats, sailboats, and other vessels of various sizes that were moored against several docks. Maple and oak trees were scattered around The Cove with pine trees further inland. While on both sides of the marina, a rugged coastline consisted of jagged rocks and forested slopes that swept down to the sea. The cliffs were peppered with rocky shores dotted with charming lighthouses, and the mountains off in the distance were breathtaking this time of year. Vibrant shades of orange, yellow, and red painted the landscape like an artist's canvas.

Washington had been a beautiful, majestic state as well, but she'd been stuck in a rut. Everything around her had reminded her of the heartbreak she'd gone through. There was something so untamed, unpredictable, and wild about northern Maine.

Right now, she could use a little excitement.

The foghorn of the ferry sounded as it left the

harbor to one of the many islands offshore, making Sparrow jump and bringing her back to the present. She shivered, giving the cold, dark, rough seas one final glance. As beautiful as the ocean was to look at, she was happy to keep her feet firmly planted on the ground.

"You ready, Sparrow?" a whiskey smooth voice said from behind her.

Greyson Adler.

She turned around and nodded, following him to the restaurant, having almost forgotten she'd agreed to have lunch with the man. He was a forest ranger and she needed information for her field project. That was the only reason she'd said yes, she told herself. She couldn't risk her heart by getting involved romantically with someone again. Not after what had happened, and especially with so many questions about that still left unanswered.

She inhaled a shaky breath and squeezed her trembling hands. Why did he have to be so beautiful. She'd met plenty of rugged, outdoorsy men in her line of work, but never one who had affected her so profoundly at first sight.

He was mesmerizing.

Well over six feet tall, and perfectly proportioned muscles filled out his green and black uniform to perfection. Thick, honey brown curls covered his head, and hypnotic eyes, a mix of brown and green swirls, unsettled her every time he looked at her. His rugged jawline, sporting a cleft in his chin, and full lips that smiled way too often had her staring at his mouth far too many times, making her forget her own mind.

"How about the table in the corner?" He stopped walking to face her and pointed across the room.

She had to catch herself before she bounced off his chest. "Wherever you want to sit is fine with me."

He gave her an amused look, nodded, and then

walked toward their table. Moving her eyes to safer territory, she looked around The Claw as she followed him to their seats.

The waterfront pub had a nautical theme with pictures of the catch of the day on the wall. Fishing boat captains and their crews, a few residents she'd met, as well as what looked to be fall tourists filled the restaurant for lunch. Dim lighting lent itself to a cozy atmosphere as classic rock filtered through the sound system and a reality TV fishing show played out on a big screen above the bar.

It was charming. Sparrow could see why people spoke so highly of it.

A man with thick, dirty blond hair and sea green eyes set two menus down in front of them.

"Hey, Jack, looks like you have a full crowd today." Greyson glanced around the pub full of regulars and tourists.

Jack nodded. "Between the fall festivals, leaf peepers, and hunters, The Cove is packed. But I'm not complaining. You know how things are around here in the winter."

"A ghost town."

"Exactly." The blond man grinned, then turned his gaze on her. "I see you made a new friend." His tone held a teasing note.

"Ha-ha." Greyson arched a thick brow high, responding wryly, "I do have a few of those, you know."

"You'd never know it." Jack chuckled." All I've ever seen you do is work."

Greyson rolled his eyes. "Anyway, Jack Ross, meet Wildlife Biologist Sparrow James. Sparrow, Jack is the owner of this fine establishment, as well as a firefighter, and he runs a snowplow operation."

"Wow, you really are a jack of all trades." Sparrow

smiled wide and held out her hand. "It's very nice to meet you."

Jack laughed. "Trust me. Around these parts, most of us wear many hats, especially in the winter. You can count on your neighbors looking out for each other, that's for sure." He shook her hand. "It's a pleasure to meet you. The women are going to love you, especially my girlfriend, Zoe. Unlike this one," he jerked his head toward Greyson, "I don't doubt for a minute that you'll have any problems making friends."

"You gonna take our order, or what?" Greyson shook his head, but a small smile played at the corners of his lips.

Jack took Greyson's menu from him. "I don't know why you bother looking at a menu when you order the same thing every time."

"I can't help it. Your mother's Clam Chowder is unmatched in all of New England. And the warm buttery homemade rolls are mouthwatering."

"You've got that right." Jack looked at Sparrow. "And for the lovely lady?"

"Well, after that description, I'll take the same."

"Good choice." Jack winked. "Care for anything to drink?"

Greyson looked at his watch. "Considering I'm still on duty, make mine coffee."

"Just an iced tea for me, please."

"Done." Jack took Sparrow's menu and headed for the kitchen.

"What a nice man." Sparrow's gaze skimmed the pub. "I really like the people around here so far."

"Jack's a regular charmer. Or he used to be, until Zoe Granger stole his heart. She was a sheriff's deputy but recently became the new Harbormaster. Formerly part of the Coast Guard, this job suits her perfectly. She and the sheriff's wife Stacy—who's our sports journalist —are best friends. Actually, there's a group of them. The mayor, Laura; that realtor, Tia, I was telling you about; and our local medical examiner, Olivia, are all pretty tight. Jack's sister Emma is part of their group whenever she's home. She's a storm chaser, so she's gone a lot and lives in Virginia with her fiancé, Gunner."

"Wow, what an interesting group of women. I can't wait to meet them all. I haven't had a group of girlfriends in a long time." Sparrow played with the napkin in front of her, trying not to squirm under his stare. "Too long."

Jack brought their soup and rolls over to them, saving her from having to go into more detail. "Enjoy," he said and then walked away.

Sparrow and Greyson ate in silence.

The rich soup, filled with tender potatoes and juicy lumps of clam swimming in a pool of thick cream, brought her tastebuds to life. A moan of pleasure slipped out of her mouth, and she blinked.

Greyson's eyes crinkled at the corners, and he raised his spoon in salute, nodding his head in agreement, as his mouth was full of the heavenly dish.

Light and fluffy rolls called her name. They were topped with a thick layer of buttery goodness that melted in her mouth after dipping them in the soup.

When they were finished, they spent the next hour talking about maps of the area, the places she wanted to conduct her research, hunting season, and poachers. She had a lot more planning to do and equipment to gather before she would be ready, but she felt more informed after talking to him.

"I can't thank you enough, Greyson. This information has been a big help." She smiled at him.

"You're very welcome. That's what our departments are for. Working together to preserve and protect the plants and animals in these woods." He smiled back. "Anything at all you might need, don't hesitate to ask."

"I just might take you up on that."

"Name the time and place, and it's a date."

There was that saying again. Although, the second time around, that phrase didn't seem so scary. Her heart did a funny little flip, and for the first time in a long time, she was afraid of what she might do about it. What had she gotten herself into?

* * *

LATER THAT DAY, after dropping Sparrow back at the office, Greyson headed to the woods in his company jeep with his supplies. This time of year, there were designated state lands to hunt most animals. Moose were hunted for a limited time with a special permit only, and bobcats after December. It was the undesignated lands the poachers were targeting that he was worried about the most.

Northern Maine woods were so vast, it was hard to make rounds and patrol them all frequently enough. Several forest ranger teams were making rounds daily in their assigned areas, but there simply weren't enough of them employed to do the job justice. Not to mention, these poachers were smart. They kept watch and moved around accordingly, making it difficult to catch them.

Static sounded in between voices heard over his push-to-talk, two-way radio. Rangers and game wardens checked in, as well as a few wildlife biology teams, depending on what frequency you tuned in to.

A lot of the woods could be accessed by foot or off-road motorbikes, all-terrain vehicles, and snowmobiles, depending on the time of year. There weren't a lot of roads for larger vehicles like jeeps and trucks the further one traveled inland. With the wood products industry clearing out large areas of timber, the rough logging roads made access easier, but not safer for someone inexperienced.

Greyson navigated his way through the woods, noticing the tamarack trees were beginning to drop their needles. He passed his usual check points, installing more security cameras, looking for animal traps and any sign of illegal activity. It was almost as if the poachers were one step ahead of the rangers and game wardens, always knowing the areas to avoid. They had yet to catch any of them on the hidden cameras, making their job that much more difficult.

Navigating his way further inland, Greyson drove down a rough road lined with cedar trees, intermixed with maple, beech, and many of the region's most popular trees. Through his open windows the strong scent of balsam fir and spruce filled the interior of his jeep better than any drug store air freshener.

The wood products industry did a good job managing the area along with the forest rangers, keeping illegal logging at bay and controlling wildfires. The landscape was filled with plenty of lakes, ponds, wetlands, bogs, rivers, and streams, making it a prime habitat for the existing wildlife.

With new logging roads popping up all the time, it made previously inaccessible areas available for birdwatchers. But birdwatchers weren't the only ones benefiting from them. Illegal hunters and trappers interested in poaching animals for coveted body parts and to sell to the illegal exotic pet industry used these access roads as well.

The sun set early in these parts, especially this time of year, and the afternoon dwindled away. Greyson finished patrolling the forest and started making his way back toward Coldwater Cove when movement caught his eye. Slowing his jeep to a stop on the side of the road, he scanned the area, narrowing his eyes. The object he'd seen hadn't looked like an animal. He could have sworn he'd seen a person.

"Ranger Adler here," he called out loudly. "Is anyone out there?"

Nothing.

Greyson climbed out of his jeep, keeping to the shadows and on alert. He scanned the immediate area for the familiar green tactical uniform of another ranger. When dusk settled, it was easy to get turned around if on foot. He squinted into the fading light, knowing for sure he'd seen something or someone. Was it a newly assigned ranger? Maybe a lost hiker? Or what if his jeep had surprised a poacher?

Greyson needed to be sure.

With a determined sigh, he grabbed the long, heavy Maglite from the charger in the jeep and slipped it through the flashlight ring hanging on his belt next to his baton and pepper spray. Checking another pouch, he tested a smaller tactical flashlight, making sure its bright LED bulb worked, and then he unhooked the snap over the top of his 9mm Smith & Wesson semiautomatic pistol, needing to be ready if the situation should arise.

Formerly, forest rangers weren't allowed to carry weapons. But given they were often in remote areas on their own, the need to protect themselves from criminals and wild animals had become a must over the years. Thankfully, the state had agreed and passed a law reflecting as much.

He ventured into the woods, clearing brush out of his way as he walked, keeping behind the trees as cover. A strong sensation of being watched settled over him. Given the nature of his job, that sensation could be from man or animal. He shined a flashlight with one hand, keeping the other hand at the ready over his weapon. The wind whipped up, stirring a pile of pine needles and leaves on the forest floor into a mini tornado before the debris fluttered back to the damp earth.

Walking for several more yards, he finally came to a stop and listened. No footsteps, just normal sounds of the woods. Birds fluttering and singing, small animals scurrying about, leaves rustling from the wind blowing through the trees.

Nothing ominous or out of the ordinary.

With one more look around the area, he decided to turn back. Whatever it was, it had apparently lost interest and was long gone. Left with no alternative, Greyson headed back to his jeep. Looking ahead, he squinted. Stopping abruptly, he glanced down and squatted by the ground.

Boot prints.

Pulling out his cellphone, he took a picture of the tread pattern, and then stood to walk a few more steps. Stopping once more, he noticed something else on the ground.

"What do we have here?" Crouching down again, he pulled on a pair of rubber gloves then picked up a bullet casing and tried not to grind his teeth.

Poachers.

Something wasn't right. An odd feeling nagged at his gut. He held the casing up and inspected it closer in the waning light for several moments before dropping it into a plastic bag. He looked around the area one last time as he stood. His mouth formed a frown as one thought plagued his brain...

That shell did not belong to any hunting rifle he'd ever seen.

3

THE NEXT MORNING, Sparrow walked into The Lost Horizon for breakfast. The place was a quaint diner just down the road from her hotel with scenic pictures of The Cove in all four seasons. Victoria and Chris had both told her it was the best breakfast place in town, especially since it was under new management.

She bumped into a man around her father's age, with a salt and pepper buzz cut, hunting gear on, and a wide smile. "Oh, I'm so sorry," she said.

"Careful, ma'am. I wouldn't want you to get hurt on account of me." He glanced around at the crowded diner. "Town's getting busy with hunting season and fall activities resuming." He glanced at his watch. "Speaking of which, I need to get going if I'm going to get a good spot before dusk. I didn't have much luck this morning. Hoping to bag a moose this year." He tipped his head. "Have a nice day and try the pancakes. They're to die for."

"Thanks for the tip." She smiled back and waved as he headed out the door. Everyone in this town was so friendly. She glanced around for a place to sit when a woman who looked like she could be the centerfold for Ms. Fitness Magazine came charging over to her.

"You must be the new wildlife biologist, Sparrow James." The woman wore her platinum blonde wavy hair in a low bun, had a khaki uniform with a harbormaster patch on, and a pair of duck boots as she stared at Sparrow with excited ice-blue eyes.

"You would be right." Sparrow smiled back at the woman. "And you must be Zoe Granger."

"I sure am." She wrinkled her brow. "How'd you know?"

"Your harbormaster patch. Jack told me about you, and Ranger Adler told me where you work."

"That's right, Jack said you and Greyson had lunch at The Claw yesterday." Zoe took Sparrow by the arm. "Come with me. I want you to meet my friends."

Having no choice to do anything else, Sparrow followed along slightly behind Zoe as she charged forward until they came to a table with a group of women.

"We saved a seat in case you showed up. It doesn't take a long time of living in The Cove to hear The Lost Horizon is the best place to go for breakfast." The petite blonde, with hair like Tinker Bell and lavender eyes, held out her hand. "I'm Mayor Baker-Flemming, but you can call me Laura."

"It's so nice to meet you. I don't meet many people as short as me." Sparrow smiled genuinely, feeling a connection with this woman. She was maybe five-foot-two at the most where Sparrow just made the five-foot mark.

"Agreed. It's hard for us pixies to be taken seriously." Laura adjusted the collar on her deep red suit coat. The powerful color was fitting for the fall and looked fantastic on the petite dynamo.

"Isn't that the truth." Sparrow pondered her own career. People never thought a woman her size could make it in the wild doing field work. They always tried to protect her even though she'd spent years learning how to protect herself, becoming proficient in self-defense and earning her black belt in jiu-jitsu. Ironically, it was usually her being the one to protect them.

Having to earn respect every single time got old and more than a little frustrating.

"Well, let me tell you, tall girls like me feel the pressure, too." A tall woman with crazy curly auburn hair, amber eyes, and a smooth, radio-talk-show voice chimed in. "You ladies might have to constantly prove you can do anything anyone else can, where I am *expected* to be able to do *everything* just because of my height. It's a lot to live up to."

"I hear you." Another tall woman with buzzed blonde hair, caramel skin, honey brown eyes, and gorgeous model looks gave the other woman a high five. "My parents have such high expectations for me in the family business. I'm not allowed to make mistakes like my brothers." Her gaze landed on Sparrow. "I'm Tia Johnson, and this Amazon goddess is Stacy Buchanan-West. She's a world class swimmer turned sports journalist when she's not on maternity leave, and my family runs a real estate business. Let me know if you need help finding a better place to live than the hotel."

"I just might take you up on that when I finish my field work," Sparrow said to Tia, then her gaze settled on Stacy, and she forced her eyes not to drop to the woman's stomach as she pushed the lump in her throat down. "How old's your baby?"

"She's two weeks old today. Lizzie, named after my late mother, Elizabeth. Today is my first day out of the house. My husband, Trent, is the sheriff. He took the morning off just so I could have some 'me' time with my girls. I really am so glad you could join us."

"Me too. Do you have a picture of your daughter?"

Stacy dug her cellphone out of her purse and

beamed as she showed several pictures of a beautiful baby girl with dark hair.

Sparrow's heart melted and she smiled tenderly. "She's precious."

"She might look like her daddy, but her feisty cry tells me she's gonna be just like her mama." Stacy couldn't stop beaming proudly. "I love the little peanut, but I am not complaining about some alone time right now. Who knew having a baby would be so much work with very little sleep?"

"Me!" Laura laughed. "Try having twin girls. Talk about work." Her smile dimmed. "Life was crazy busy when they were little, but I worked as the town clerk. When I left my job at the end of the day, I could focus on my family. My husband, Tommy, owns his own car dealership, so he's always been busy. I used to pick up the slack back then. But as the girls grew older, they required less work. So, when the opportunity came along for me to run for mayor, I took it."

"Because you deserve it," Stacy said. "It's your time to shine. You sacrificed a lot, now it's your turn to be in the spotlight."

"I agree, but I can't leave my job when I get home from the office, and Tommy is the one who is picking up the slack these days. The girls swim year-round now, and this time of year, their practices are earlier at the indoor pool. He has more flexibility than I do to take them, but he's not happy about it."

"I remember those days when you and I swam together. The smell of chlorine, the feel of the ripples from the water against our skin, our hair tucked into bathing caps. I miss it sometimes." Stacy smiled, looking nostalgic.

"Me, too. That's why I wish I could be there more often. The girls are growing up so fast. I feel like I'm missing it all."

Stacy reached out and squeezed Laura's hand. "Hang in there, mama. Things will get better. Did you hire more help?"

"Yes, and during the summer, things seemed a little better between us. I had a little more time with Tommy and the girls, but now the fall festival season is picking up. I'm busier than ever. Between the Nature Craft Festival, the Lobsterman Triathlon, Open Lighthouse Day, the Harvest Festival, and Octoberfest, there's little time left over. Then throw in the leaf peepers arriving in droves to see the fall leaves, and Coldwater Cove is swamped. I'm not complaining. The town can always use the profit that brings. It just makes my life even crazier, and my marriage less stable."

"At least we haven't had any more murders to deal with since last spring." Another petite woman with jet black silky hair that fell to her shoulders and eyes a darker stormy gray than Sparrow's joined them.

Laura sighed. "There is that at least." She looked at Sparrow. "Sorry to put a downer on the morning."

"Hey, no worries," Sparrow replied. "We all have our struggles." She'd been in therapy for two years because of hers, but she wasn't ready to open up to strangers about the details of her troubles just yet.

"Well, I for one am sick of worrying about things I can't control. Onward and upward to brighter things. Like introducing you to our lovely medical examiner, Dr. Olivia Jones. Olivia, meet Sparrow, the new wildlife biologist."

Olivia's eyes brightened. "Ah, Hank told me all about you. He's my boyfriend and the chief of police. You haven't met him yet, but you know how things go in a small town. Everyone knows who you are already. Trent and Hank hang out with Greyson and Jack a lot."

"Tommy and Trent used to hang out more, but the busier I get, the less social Tommy becomes. I feel bad and tell him we can hire a sitter, but he never takes me up on it. I don't know what to do anymore."

"Have you tried marriage counseling?" Stacy took a sip of coffee.

Laura shrugged. "I mentioned it, but I doubt Tommy will go. Maybe Trent can talk to him."

"It's worth a shot." Stacy lifted one shoulder.

"Enough about me." Laura pasted on a smile that didn't quite reach her eyes and turned to Sparrow. "You'll want to meet the maintenance man, Larry Shaw. He's the town's handyman because he pretty much fixes anything that breaks in Coldwater Cove. He's gotten so busy, he's hired an assistant named Buck."

"Good to meet you, Olivia," Sparrow said, "and thanks for the tip about Larry and Buck, Laura. I might be a MacGyver in the field with natural resources, but give me anything man-made, and I struggle. Cars, kitchen appliances, anything electrical…it's not pretty."

They all laughed then took a moment to order breakfast from their waiter, made small talk, and ate their meals in silence. Their orders had come quickly, the service was exceptional, and the food was delicious.

Sparrow set her fork down. "Well, I guess I'd better head into the office. I have a big field project to finish planning." She pulled her wallet out of the small backpack she always carried, dropping cash on the table.

"Anything exciting?" Stacy asked. "I'm living through all of you ladies for the next four weeks until I can go back to work."

"Don't rush it. I would give anything to be at home with a sweet baby like yours." Sparrow blinked. She hadn't meant to reveal that, but these ladies were so easy to talk to. They all stared at her curiously. "Meanwhile," she quickly continued, "I'll be restoring habitats along with researching any birds that move inland for the winter." She shrugged. "Just boring bird stuff."

"Sounds exciting to me," Stacy said with a grin.

"Sounds dangerous to me," Laura added with a frown.

"It's okay. I won't be alone. I have an assistant and skills on how to handle myself in the woods."

"Greyson's not just a forest ranger," Olivia chimed in. "He's an expert survivalist. I'm sure he can help you with whatever you need."

"He already has." Sparrow gathered her backpack and stood. "I really do have to go. It was lovely to meet you all. It's been a while since I've had friends." She had parents, a brother, and a sister back home in Washington, but her friends had abandoned her.

Drinking heavily tends to make a person lose a lot of things.

"We take care of each other around here." Tia handed Sparrow her business card. "Just know you're not alone. You're a part of our group now, and I really do just want to help get you settled."

Sparrow took the card with a genuine smile. "Thank you, ladies. This means more than you know. And, well, you're kind of stuck with me now." She shrugged. "If I stick around long term, that is."

"Oh, I have a feeling we'll be seeing you for the long haul. People who move here don't usually leave. The Cove has a way of giving people exactly what they need no matter what they start out looking for." Laura smiled tenderly at Sparrow.

They all did, as if they could see clear into her soul.

Sparrow nodded once, unable to talk past the lump in her throat, then gave the ladies a wave as she headed out the door. She was so emotional these days. The only thing she was looking for was a fresh start. She had no idea what she needed…

But she had a feeling she was about to find out.

* * *

"SHERIFF WEST." Greyson shook Trent's hand outside the gun club. "Chief Masters." He shook Hank's hand next. "Glad I caught you both."

Greyson had stopped by their offices and was told they were both investigating a heated dispute at Coldwater Cove Gun Club. A local hunter named Greggor was there to sight in his gun and a tourist named Nigel was obviously there to cause trouble as an anti-gun birdwatching naturalist.

The rifle range was outside, and the pistol range was inside so the club was open year-round. They also had a bar and restaurant for members only. Apparently, the tourist wouldn't take no for an answer, complaining about discrimination, demanding someone serve him a drink and a meal.

And the member, who'd had one too many, was having none of it. Greggor reeked of gun powder and alcohol, while Nigel smelled like antiseptic. The sheriff and chief had separated the two men into each of their squad cars and were about to leave.

"Good to see you in one piece, Ranger Adler." Trent lifted his wide-brimmed, dark brown hat to scrub a hand over his brown buzz cut then run it over his whiskered jaw. His brow scrunched up over concerned hazel eyes. "I heard about the poachers. This isn't the time to be short a game warden."

Trent was a former marine turned FBI agent before marrying a local legendary swimmer and becoming the new sheriff.

"Wanda says the higher ups are working on getting us all more help." Greyson shook his head and donned his green cap. "Trouble is getting people willing to live in such a harsh place during the winter."

Hank was a former FBI profiler before moving to I

Cove with the medical examiner and becoming the new chief of police. He adjusted his black peaked hat over his blond hair and blue eyes, his dimples sinking deep as his mouth flattened into a straight line.

Hank nodded. "This will be my first winter here, and I have to say I'm not exactly looking forward to it. But the rest of the seasons make living in The Cove worthwhile. Let me make some calls to my contacts in Boston. They may know someone qualified who might be interested in relocating to this area."

"I appreciate that." Greyson tipped his hat before settling it back on his head. "I wanted to check with both of you on the shell casing I found on my rounds in the woods." He pulled out his phone and showed them a picture. "Have either of you seen a casing like this?"

"Did you send it off to NIBIN?" Hank studied the image.

NIBIN was the National Integrated Ballistic Information Network. "I submitted it late yesterday, but I haven't received the ballistic report yet."

"Looks like it could be from a sniper rifle." Trent frowned. "You say you found that in the woods?"

Greyson nodded. "A remote area not used by hunters."

Trent narrowed his eyes. "You thinking poachers?"

"They have been venturing further inland. They keep changing their location, and so far, we haven't been able to capture them on camera."

"Let us know if you need any help." Hank looked at the men in their cars. "This is the most excitement we've had in The Cove in a while."

"Careful what you wish for." Greyson slid his phone in his pocket. "I'll definitely give you a buzz if anything turns up. What are you going to do with those two?"

"Keep them separated until they both cool off. Trent will bring Greggor home to sleep it off, and I'll bring

Nigel back to his hotel. I told him any more trouble out of him, and I'll be happy to escort him across the county line."

"I'm with Hank. You need any help, feel free to give us a shout."

"Will do." Greyson saluted the men.

Trent's phone rang and he glanced at the caller ID. "Excuse me, gentlemen. I have to take this." He walked off for privacy.

"What was that all about?" Greyson looked at Hank in confusion.

"I have no clue." Hank shrugged. "I'm sure if Trent had something relevant to share, he would."

"Fair enough. I'll catch up with you later." Greyson headed back to his office, hoping for an email with a report waiting for him.

This poaching was getting out of control. Something kept nagging at his gut. He couldn't place what was wrong, but something was definitely off. And he'd always trusted his gut. Not to mention, he didn't like the idea of a certain gray-eyed, burgundy-haired little songbird heading out into the woods to do a field study.

He wasn't worried about her surviving the elements and the wildlife. What concerned him was the unknown. Hunters venturing into areas they weren't supposed to, and ruthless poachers willing to do just about anything to snag their prize.

He had to do something...

Problem was, he didn't have a damn clue what.

4

I STOOD inside the Coldwater Cove Mini-mart gas station in the center of town, watching Sparrow and Lily fill their truck and the two four-wheelers on the trailer behind it up with gas. I narrowed my eyes, trying to see into the back. It looked like she'd packed enough belongings for a month, which told me she was about to start her field project.

Keeping track of what was going on in The Cove was essential.

All sorts of biologists, rangers, and game wardens frequented the woods. That was to be expected and un-avoidable in northern Maine. If I were honest, at first it had made what I was doing that much more exciting. Lately I was worried things might have gone too far, but I couldn't stop. I was in too deep and had too much to lose.

Whatever the cost, I couldn't get caught.

I clenched my teeth, still staring out the store win-dow, and forced myself to take a few deep breaths and relax before someone saw me acting strangely. I hated this time of year. The Cove was too damn busy for my liking.

Sparrow had pulled off to the side in a parking spot.

Moments later, Ranger Greyson Adler pulled into the spot beside her. My heart sped up as I watched him carry something to her window and hand it to her, then they fell into a deep conversation.

Something about this new woman disturbed me.

Probably because I'd seen her a few too many times with Greyson. I'd never liked the guy. He was laser focused on looking for his parents. The man had a habit of venturing deeper into the woods than he had any right to and sticking his nose in other people's business where it didn't belong. I didn't need this woman getting any crazy ideas about exploring areas she had no business being in, either. She needed to stick to her field site area and stay put.

My gut turned sour.

I didn't like violence, but I wasn't afraid to do what I had to in order to stop others from ruining everything. Someone called my name, jerking me from my thoughts. I pasted on a smile before turning around and playing the game.

* * *

SPARROW TOOK the maps from Greyson and smiled. "Thank you. I appreciate the highlights and notes you made."

He shrugged, running a hand through his honey brown curls before resting his hat on his head. "My notes are up to date and probably more thorough than the average map." The green in his brown eyes was more pronounced today as he stared intently at her. "Be careful out there. Hunters shouldn't be in the area you're headed to, but then again, poachers really don't give a damn about rules. It's also mating season for moose, and bears are fattening up for winter. You'll want to steer clear of both."

"Don't worry. I have all the tools I need to ward off any threat. I can take care of myself, Ranger." Sparrow tried not to sigh. Would he have worried about a male biologist? Biting her tongue, she added, "This isn't my first time in the field. Washington woods aren't exactly a walk in the park, you know."

"True, but northern Maine can be exceptionally harsh and bear spray alone won't stop a bullet. No one really understands until they experience it firsthand just how harsh this area is with the unpredictable weather conditions and being so close to the vast Canadian border." Greyson's eyes softened as he studied her.

"Well, Washington is also right up against Canada." She thrust her chin up and tried not to squirm.

"Your face is very expressive, Ms. James." His lips twitched at the corners. "It doesn't matter if you are a man or a woman. I would give the same warning to anyone heading into these woods, especially with the suspicious activity and shortage of staffing we have going on at the moment."

Sparrow felt her cheeks flush with heat, but she refused to look away. "Understood. I'll heed your warning and take the proper precautions."

"And she has me," Lily chimed in, flipping her long thick blue braid over her shoulder. "I've been in these woods countless times, plus I have my concealed carry." She patted the bump beneath her jacket and winked. "Something tells me we'll be just fine."

"Duly noted." Greyson nodded and tapped the top of their truck. "Good luck, ladies. I'm just a radio call away if you need anything."

Sparrow nodded once then pulled out of the parking lot and headed toward the edge of town where she would take the logging road to her destination.

Looking behind her in the rear-view mirror, she did a double take and sucked in a sharp breath.

Harlow?

A man stood on the sidewalk in front of the gas station, staring at her car. She blinked to clear her vision, but no one was there. Maybe he'd ducked into the store. If she weren't running late, she would turn around and check to be sure she wasn't losing her mind. Had she imagined him? It would make sense. She had done that before.

That was what had gotten her into trouble.

"Watch out," Lily blurted. "You're headed off the road."

Sparrow looked straight ahead as she jerked the truck back between the lines on the pavement, the trailer swaying wildly behind them. She cleared her throat and kept her eyes firmly locked on the road in front of her. "Sorry."

"Are you okay?" She could feel Lily studying her, and the concern in her voice couldn't be missed.

That was the million-dollar question.

Was she okay? Sparrow wasn't entirely sure. She would need to call her therapist as soon as her field work was over. "I'm fine," she finally managed to say, belying her shaky voice. "I just thought I saw someone from my past, but that's not possible. It can't be."

"Really? Why not?"

Her heart ached like it always did when she thought about what had happened. She couldn't go there, so she inhaled deeply and replied, "Because he went missing almost two years ago."

A heavy pause settled between them.

"Oh, no. I'm so sorry," Lily finally responded, adding softly, "who was he?"

"My fiancé."

Sparrow knew her tone left no question that she

didn't want to talk about it, and thankfully, Lily seemed to understand. She didn't ask any more questions for the rest of the ride through the woods.

Finally, they reached the pull-off where they would leave the truck and take the ATVs the rest of the way. They climbed out of the vehicle and loaded their supplies onto small trailers they kept in a shack for that purpose. Heading out again, it was a good thirty minutes before they would reach their destination.

Sparrow took in her surroundings as she led the way. So far, the weather had cooperated. Rays of sunshine were streaming through the tops of massive balsam fir, spruce, tamarack, and cedar trees mixed in with vibrant red, orange, and yellow maple, beech, and birch trees. The rays created an impressive light show as the breeze blew through the tree branches, making them dance about.

Small critters scampered up and down trees, across the forest floor, and behind rocks. The ground was littered with pinecones and pine needles as well as colorful leaves. The landscape was well-watered with lots of lakes, streams, and rivers that made for a prime wildlife habitat.

Traveling deeper into the woods, they broke through a clearing with a large meadow filled with lingering wildflowers that would die off before winter. The parks that most residents and tourists frequented were closer to the coast and ended along a rocky cliff overlooking the sea, but the Maine woods inland were just as breathtaking...

And even more dangerous.

Merging back into the trees, they were almost at their destination when she saw a flash of movement through the trees. Her heart sped up over the thought of fending off a bear or moose. Another flash of movement happened, and she frowned.

She studied the trees closer with squinted eyes but saw nothing. She could have sworn she saw camo clothing and long hair. Unless bears wore clothing or bigfoot was out there, the movement had to have come from a human being. No one was supposed to be in this area. Hunters were confined to certain areas, and bird-watchers or leaf peepers kept to certain areas as well.

Maybe the culprit was part of the poaching Greyson had warned her about.

When no more movements happened, she started wondering if she really was losing her mind. Shaking off that disturbing thought, she focused on the trail until they finally reached their destination a short time later.

Sparrow blinked.

What the hell was going on today? A tent was set up already. She cut the engine to her ATV and checked her map to make sure she had the right location. She was definitely in the right spot.

They, however, were *not*.

Looking at Lily, she raised her brows. "Do you know if anyone else was supposed to be here?"

Lily shrugged. "Chris didn't say anything about anyone else being here." She frowned as she studied the logo on the side of the tent. "That is definitely not one of ours."

"Have you heard of Conservation Consultants?"

Lily was already shaking her head. "It has to be a private lab, but usually they're hired by businesses along the coast. I have no idea what their interest could be this far inland."

"That's what I'm wondering." Sparrow frowned. Climbing off her ATV, she headed over to the tent.

"Where are you going?" Lily looked around nervously.

"To get some answers." Sparrow forged ahead with Lily hot on her heels.

Walking all around the tent, there was no one there. The women ventured into the woods, keeping their eyes peeled, but didn't see anything. When they returned a little while later, they saw two men going through Sparrow and Lily's supplies attached to their trailers.

Lily stopped short and unzipped her jacket, her hand hovering above her weapon.

"Hey, what do you think you're doing?" Sparrow marched over to the men before Lily had a chance to do something she might regret.

One man was tall and thin with auburn hair parted on the side and expensive glasses perched on his nose. The other man was shorter with an athletic build. He had slicked back mahogany colored hair, and a clean-shaven square jaw.

"I could ask you the same question," the shorter more muscular one said with a thick French accent as he took a step toward her.

"We're not the ones going through your stuff." Lily's hand twitched.

Sparrow didn't own a gun. She preferred to use her hands and mind to defend herself. "The state of Maine gives us the right to be here. Can you say the same?"

The taller man held up his hands and spoke with a smooth, calm tone. "Let's start over, shall we?" He smiled and held out his hand. "I'm Wildlife Biologist Ozzy Price, and this is my assistant, Peter LaCroix."

"Like the water?" Lily asked with a smirk.

Peter quirked a brow but did *not* reach out his hand.

Sparrow narrowed her eyes, studying them both before shaking Ozzy's hand. He wasn't like any biologist she'd ever met. He didn't smell like a science lab like her. "I'm Wildlife Biologist Sparrow James, and this is my assistant, Lily Brown."

Lily crossed her arms, arching her own brow.

"We work for the Maine Department of Conservation." Sparrow pointed to the logo on her jacket and then glanced at their logo free clothing. "I take it you work for Conservation Consultants." She pointed at their tent.

Ozzy nodded. "Yes, we're a private lab, hired by companies with conservation issues. We're new to northern Maine, but we've worked up and down the east coast for years."

"What are you doing this far inland?" Sparrow watched him closely.

"That's confidential per my client's request." Ozzy smiled, but it didn't quite reach his eyes.

He was competitive, but then again, so was she when it came to her research projects. "Well, it was a pleasure meeting you, but according to the state, I am scheduled to do field work in this area, and you are not. You'll have to pack up your belongings and cover a different part of the woods." Sparrow held his gaze. "But I would check with the state to make sure you're cleared to work an area first. I would hate for your company to get into trouble for interfering with anyone else's field work for the state."

A muscle in Peter's jaw pulsed as he looked at Ozzy with questions in his eyes.

Ozzy tilted his head once. "No problem. I will check with my boss. We never venture into the field without clearance. I'm sure it was a simple miscommunication somewhere." He looked at Peter and gestured toward their tent. "We'll be out of your way momentarily." Ozzy walked over to join Peter in packing up their gear.

"I don't trust them," Lily said once they were out of

earshot. "Especially the shorter one. Why were they going through our stuff? I bet they would steal our research if given the chance. We'll have to watch out for them. Make sure they don't come back."

"I got the same vibe. As long as they leave us alone, they're not our problem. In the meantime, let's unpack our gear."

The men finished loading the last of their supplies onto their own ATVs. Ozzy said something to Peter who fired up his engine and left the opposite way that Sparrow and Lily had come in. They must be catching a different logging road.

Ozzy suddenly turned to look Sparrow in the eye. He smiled pleasantly. "Be careful, ladies. I hear the woods can be dangerous this time of year." He fired up his engine and took off before she had a chance to respond.

5

SPARROW AND LILY spent the rest of the day setting up their tent then collecting samples from the habitat. Suddenly, large, puffy cumulus clouds rolled in, and the sky darkened. The wind abruptly changed direction, causing a sudden drop in temperature and atmospheric pressure. The smell of rain hung heavy in the air. A loud boom of thunder sounded in the distance.

Sparrow looked at Lily. "I don't like the sound of that." It was fall, but a late thunderstorm was still possible.

"Me either. Damn weather is so unpredictable here." Lily frowned.

"I'm beginning to see that." Sparrow glanced at the sky through the swaying trees. "Let's head back to base-camp. We don't have time to make it to the truck, and the last thing we need is to get caught in a thunder-storm on the ATVs."

"Agreed."

The emergency weather radio they'd brought with them sounded a warning a little too late. After quickly making it back to camp and storing their supplies, they sheltered inside on rubber sleeping mats and hoped for the best as the first fat raindrops began to fall.

There had been no storms predicted when Sparrow had set up their tent. Still, she was always prepared. She'd purposely chosen a location that was on lower ground. Lightning tended to travel along whatever path got it to the ground the quickest, so tall conductive objects got hit first.

She'd made sure their tent wasn't the only thing in the clearing. Yet she'd also made sure they weren't directly beneath a tall tree. She'd chosen some shorter cover to provide the best possible safety measures just in case the weather turned bad. Now she was grateful that she had taken those precautions.

A gust of wind shook their tent hard, and the rain came down heavier. "You secured the guy lines, right?" Sparrow asked Lily. Tents came with guy lines, and Sparrow always used them all. She'd learned the hard way it was better to be safe than sorry.

"Yes, and I made sure the rain fly was taut." Lily donned her raingear.

Sparrow had already put on hers, anticipating a long night.

Thunderstorms could cause downburst winds which swept through strong and fast, sometimes more than one hundred miles per hour. If the tent wasn't secure, it could be ripped away, and that would be disastrous with them inside. Thunderstorms could intensify quickly, so they sat silently, staying alert.

Over the next hour, the rain continued with heavy torrential downpours. Neither woman could sleep, but voicing their concern made the danger of their situation a little too alarming. Most people feared lightning from thunderstorms, but the real danger was being exposed to the elements. The risk of hypothermia was very real, especially this time of year.

Sparrow closed her eyes. Why was this happening on her first day in the field?

She always referred to the COLD method to prevent hypothermia: cleanliness, avoiding overheating, layers, and dryness. Keep your layer of clothing clean to enhance the insulation effect, adjust your layers as well as your sleeping bag to avoid overheating through sweating and losing body heat, and keep your clothing loose and dry so as not to restrict blood flow so the body stayed insulated.

Staying dry was definitely the most important aspect of hypothermia prevention, making rain gear a must, especially during a storm. Sparrow was no novice. She'd packed plenty of loose layers and had instructed Lily to do so as well, even though Lily was no novice, either. Even after all that, Sparrow shivered from the drop in temperatures.

Not a good sign.

Suddenly, a bright flash of lightning streaked across the sky, lighting up the inside of their tent. A second later, they heard a sizzling crack followed by a boom of thunder that shook the ground hard. The sound of splitting wood was unmistakable.

Sparrow looked at Lily and yelled, "Run!"

Ripping a hole in the tent with a nearby knife, they managed to make it out and scramble to a safe distance just in time. A massive tree she had thought was far enough away from their tent split high above the ground from a direct lightning strike. Tightening their raincoats and hoods against the pelting rain, they watched as if in slow motion.

A huge branch, commonly known as a widow-maker, broke off and started falling to the ground, picking up speed along the way. The high winds blew it directly toward their tent as it came plummeting to the ground until it finally crashed on top of it, rattling the earth.

That was too close.

Lily looked at Sparrow in shock. Sparrow had to focus and remain clearheaded. They couldn't stay idle out in the open where they were vulnerable. She had to do something. The ground started to pool with water from the fallen tree creating a dam situation, heightened by the heavy rain. They couldn't risk the area flooding.

"We need to get to higher ground and find shelter," Sparrow shouted over the wind and rain.

Lily snapped out of her daze and shook off the shock. "This far inland we won't find any sugar shanties or hunting cabins," Lily shouted back, the first inkling of real fear sweeping over her face.

Sparrow knew this wasn't the time to panic, but they had to reach shelter and get dry fast. They were losing too much heat too quickly. They only had one option. "Then let's look for a cave."

"B-But all our supplies are in the tent beneath the tree. We don't have a radio or my gun or anything." Hysteria bubbled just beneath the surface of Lily's voice.

Sparrow used a calm but firm tone. "We'll be okay. Stick close to me, and we'll look for a cave."

She didn't want to think about what might be hiding in any cave this time of year, but what choice did they have? Not only were they vulnerable to hypothermia, but standing out in the open put them at risk for side flashes of lightning as it jumped from the object it struck to other objects in the area.

Sparrow headed deeper into the woods. She needed to find a cave below the timberline. Floods were extremely dangerous near rivers and streams from the mountains. The water could rise with little to no warning, and the consequences could be disastrous.

At the moment, hypothermia was their biggest risk of death, second only to lightning.

No pressure, Sparrow thought.

She'd been through a lot in her past. Flashes of a field assignment a couple years ago threatened to consume her. She and her fiancé had been doing work in the field similar to this. They didn't have to deal with surviving a storm, but they'd had a run-in with a wounded Grizzly. Sparrow had been trained in wilderness survival. That didn't matter one bit when faced with an angry beast.

She'd panicked and took off running instead of curling into a ball.

Her fiancé started shouting like a maniac at the same time and ran in a different direction to distract the bear, who chased him instead. He'd saved her life for sure. It was his life she wasn't so sure about. They'd both disappeared into the woods, and she hadn't seen or heard from him since.

They'd looked for almost two weeks, but search and rescue hadn't found a thing. Sparrow blamed herself, especially after she'd discovered she was pregnant. Guilt and stress eventually caused her to miscarry, and that had caused her to turn to alcohol to cope.

Not knowing what had happened to Harlow and losing his child without him ever even knowing she was pregnant was the cruelest punishment of all.

Heavy drinking had made her lose her friends, her career, and nearly her life. But she'd pulled herself together with the help of her family and her therapist. Needing a fresh start, she'd jumped at the chance to move across the country to a place her ex-fiancé had only mentioned once.

Coldwater Cove made her feel closer to him, which was probably why she thought she had seen him in town. That, and coming up on what would have been their child's first birthday, had her buying a bottle of alcohol. She'd dumped it as soon as she reached her hotel but kept the empty bottle in her room as a reminder of what not to do.

She was stronger than that.

Taking a deep breath and forging ahead, she kept repeating that mantra through her brain. Blinking past the rain, she nearly wilted with relief when she spotted a cave. As they approached the entrance, a moment of panic hit her. Her pulse picked up speed, and her mouth grew dry.

What if a bear was inside?

"Are you okay?" Lily managed to say through chattering teeth.

That snapped Sparrow out of her fear, knowing she had someone else counting on her. She looked at Lily and noticed her lips were turning blue. A newfound strength and adrenaline surged through Sparrow.

She wasn't about to fail Lily like she had Harlow and their baby.

"I'm good. Let's go." She grabbed Lily's hand and pulled her up to the cave's entrance. There was what looked like a fire that had recently been put out. Animals couldn't make fire, so she felt a sense of reassurance entering the cave. She pulled Lily the rest of the way inside but didn't see anyone.

"I wish I had my backpack. If we get out of this alive, I'm keeping my gun on me from now on." Lily squinted, trying to see ahead into the darkness.

Sparrow picked up a stick and a rock at the entrance of the dark cave. Scraping away the ends of the wet wood until she had a sharp point, she joined Lily. "We either die of the elements or face whatever might be inside. You with me?"

Lily nodded and followed closely behind Sparrow as she led the way deeper into the dark recesses of the cave. The entrance wound around to the side and Sparrow heard a noise. Oh, God, could history be repeating itself? She took a few more steps forward, then stopped short and blinked.

"What's wrong?" Lily asked.

Sparrow looked over her shoulder and motioned Lily to stay quiet and join her side, then pointed ahead.

"What's that?" Lily whispered, her brow puckering beneath her shivering.

"It's definitely not a bear," Sparrow whispered back, her eyes narrowing. "Last I checked, bears couldn't make fire. That looks like the glow of a flickering flame of some sort."

It couldn't be a fire. Everyone knew you didn't make fire inside a cave. There was nowhere for the smoke to go, not to mention the heat could cause part of the ceiling to fall. She set her jaw with determination. She could hold her own against a human being.

Lily's eyes widened. "Someone else is in here. Is that a good thing?"

Sparrow didn't take her eyes off the glow. "We're about to find out."

Slowly creeping ahead, they grew closer and closer to the glow when a form started to take shape. A man who looked like he could be Tarzan...or the Unabomber...dressed in worn-out camo clothing sat warming his hands over Sterno Green Canned Heat, candles, and an emergency stove. He had long brown hair and an equally long beard that covered most of his face, making it impossible to tell how old he was. A large pack rested against the wall, next to a bunch of branches. Some kind of meat was cooking over the stove next to a metal pitcher.

Sparrow took another step, and Lily followed suit, causing a pebble to skid across the floor. In a split second, the man surged to his feet, drew a gun, and pointed it directly at them. Sparrow sucked in a breath. So much for protecting herself.

Jiu-jitsu wouldn't stop a bullet.

* * *

GREYSON STARED at the radar flashing across the TV at The Claw. He was having dinner when the weather suddenly turned, and the National Weather Service came across the TV with a special report. A severe thunderstorm was unexpectedly bearing down upon them.

Most of the people in the waterfront pub stopped and stared.

He silently cursed.

"I could have told you that storm was a comin'. I felt it in my knees all day." Eugene, the old man of the sea, rubbed his jaw beneath his long white beard. "Gonna be a doozy. Better make sure your gal has the harbor secured, Jack."

The bar owner saluted the old man. "You don't have to worry about Zoe. She's the best harbormaster we've had in decades and Coast Guard to boot. The harbor will be just fine."

"I'm more worried about flooding on some of our low-lying roads in neighborhoods near the water," Trent said. He was having dinner with his wife, Stacy.

Stacy had told Greyson that her father, Mack, and his girlfriend, Dr. Hurn, were home from one of their many sailing adventures because he wanted to see his new granddaughter. So, they offered to babysit. Stacy's father had early onset dementia, but he was on a new trial medication that was working wonders slowing down the progression, and Doc was with him. Trent and Stacy felt fine in leaving their new baby to have their first date night since becoming parents.

Hank and his girlfriend, Olivia, happened to be dining there as well. Hank nodded in agreement. "The marina flooding will be an issue as well, if the water level rises too high. We've had a lot of rain this fall."

"That's true," Olivia said. "I've had to hold out on releasing a couple bodies due to some burials being postponed because of the weather. With winter coming, everyone's anxious to beat the first hard freeze, but that can be difficult when the ground is so saturated."

"We really need to do something about all of our roads." Laura sat with her husband, Tommy, and their twin girls at their own table. The Claw was a favorite among their friends group, and they all supported Jack as much as they could.

"Maybe you should focus on that instead of all these festivals." Tommy looked up from cutting the meat on his daughter's plates.

Greyson didn't know Tommy well, but he'd heard he had been the town's pride and joy back in the day. The high school quarterback who'd gotten a full ride to college, only to get injured and sidelined. He'd moved back home and had become the town's rockstar. With blond movie star good looks, he'd opened his own used car lot. But over the last few years since his wife had replaced him as the apple of the town's eye as mayor, he'd grown bitter and soft. Trent said they were having marital problems.

"Without the festivals, we won't have enough money to cover all the things the town needs." Laura pinched the bridge of her nose as if she had a headache.

"You can't do it all, Laura. You're not Superwoman." Tommy dug into his food, looking away from his wife.

Laura sighed.

Tommy looked up when a man with blond hair around his age came into the pub and signaled him. "I'll be right back."

"Where are you going?" Laura asked.

"I have important work, too, you know. I see a new

client of mine. He's looking to buy a car." He walked off without another word.

"I'm the most concerned about all the rangers and biologists out in the field. Most of them aren't that far inland, so they have options for various shelters they can get to." Greyson kept his eyes on the radar, steering the conversation back to the urgent matter at hand. "Sparrow and Lily don't."

"Did you try to reach them through their two-way radio?" Trent asked.

Greyson was already nodding. "I tried and the call went through, but no one answered. That makes me wonder if their radio isn't on them and why? If the weather is bad, they wouldn't still be collecting samples. They would be in their tent, taking shelter."

"Then why aren't they responding to your call?" Hank asked.

"That is the question that is bothering me the most." Greyson ran a hand through the hair on his head.

"Sparrow seemed like she knew what she was doing when we met her at breakfast the other day," Stacy said.

"What are they doing so far inland, anyway?" Olivia asked with a frown. "Seems a bit reckless if you ask me."

"A special bird project inland," Greyson said.

"She's only doing her job," Laura added with a weary tone. "Sometimes that requires going above and beyond what's normally called for."

Tommy held up his hands as he returned to their table. "Guess she's as dedicated to her job as you are," he grumbled, then tipped back the rest of his beer before sitting down.

"Sparrow is a professional," Greyson said. "I'm sure she'll be fine."

He wasn't so sure who he was trying to convince. Everyone else or himself. But the longer she went without responding to him, the more worried he got. His gut told him something was off, but there wasn't a thing he could do about it until the weather cleared, except hope for the best. This was why he didn't let himself get close to anyone. Because the minute you started to care about them, you ran the risk of getting hurt.

He couldn't handle anyone else he cared about disappearing from his life.

6

"Whoa, hey. We're not here to bother you. We're just trying to take shelter from the storm. That's all." Sparrow held her hands up high in the air as thunder boomed outside the cave, vibrating the stone beneath their feet.

Lily followed suit, looking around nervously but not saying a word.

"Anyone follow you?" the man said with a gruff voice, his eyes intense as he stared past them.

"No, it's just us," Sparrow said carefully, inhaling the earthy, musty smell surrounding her. It was damp and chilly but a hell of a lot better than facing the elements outside.

His stiff shoulders wilted slightly. "Got any weapons on you?"

"Just this." Sparrow held her sharpened branch out in front of her.

"Leave it against the wall and come in further." He lowered his gun but kept it within reach on the ground beside him.

The women slowly did as they were told and joined him by the small portable stove, grateful for any heat.

He eyed them warily. "What are you doing this far inland during a storm?"

"We're wildlife biologists." Sparrow pointed to the logo on her raincoat. "I'm Sparrow and this is Lily."

He studied the logo then tilted his head but didn't give his name.

"We were just setting up to do some field work when the storm hit unexpectedly. A tree branch came down on our tent, so all our supplies are back there. We had no choice but to look for shelter."

"These woods aren't safe," he said, but didn't elaborate.

She wanted to ask him what *he* was doing out there but didn't dare pry in case it set him off. He seemed on edge. They couldn't afford for him to kick them out. "Thank you for the hospitality."

He frowned. "You can stay the night, but then you gotta leave come dawn."

"Understood."

"W-What are you cooking?" Lily asked, her teeth chattering as she edged closer to the heat source to get warm.

"Venison. There's plenty. You need to get dry first. You can hang your wet clothes on those makeshift branches for hooks on the wall, so they'll dry out. There are blankets in plastic pouches in my pack. Help yourself to two and wrap up in them. Then come have some dinner, and I'll make you a medicinal tea."

Lily shot her a worried look, but Sparrow nodded reassuringly as she motioned for Lily to follow her to the wall. For survival's sake, Sparrow knew they needed to do as he'd instructed. They'd never warm up their core if they didn't get dry, but she also wasn't reckless. She knew she could take him if he tried anything funny.

Digging through the man's pack, she pulled out two

Emergency Thermal Mylar Blankets. Originally designed by NASA for space exploration, the compact metallicized polyethylene terephthalate material was durable and insulating. It reflected ninety percent of a person's body heat back inside them, preventing hypothermia, and was waterproof, windproof, and reusable.

While Sparrow and Lily stripped off all their wet clothing, except their undergarments, and hung them on the wall, Sparrow took stock of other items he had in his pack. Water purification tablets, green light sticks, first aid kit, emergency food bars and water pouches, solar hand crank flashlights and radio, candles and waterproof matches, duct tape, nylon cord, crowbar, safety goggles, compact trifold shovel, work gloves, and more. Clearly this man knew about survival. Who was he, and what was he doing out in the woods alone?

Or was he alone…

Sparrow felt his eyes watching her, studying her every move, so she stepped away from his pack. Handing Lily a blanket and keeping one for herself, they wrapped themselves up and felt warmer almost immediately. The man was tall and thin, but he didn't look weak. Although, if he'd wanted to hurt them, he would have tried to already.

Within moments, they were both sitting on the ground in front of the stove eating venison—most likely illegally caught since she doubted he had a hunting license and wasn't about to ask—and drinking a strong, earthy-tasting tea.

The man smelled of homeopathic medicinal herbs, all-natural homemade sunscreen, and aromatherapy oil bug spray. Nature's safe version of chemicals. Lily turned up her nose at the smell, saying she wasn't a fan of any tea, and chose hot water instead.

A little while later, after finishing their meal and sitting in thankful-to-be-alive silence, their violent shivering began to subside.

Sparrow studied the man. "Can I ask what you're doing out in the woods alone?"

"No." He drank from a water bottle, with his eyes never leaving hers.

She held up her hands. "Sorry. I wasn't trying to pry. I just thought maybe you were lost and needed help. I have a two-way radio back in our tent I could probably get for you tomorrow if I can remove enough branches to reach it."

He was already shaking his head. "Don't need your help. Just want to be left alone. Forget you ever saw me, and we'll be square." His intense gaze burned into Sparrow, making his message clear. He wasn't asking.

Sparrow shrugged. "Suit yourself."

"That's fair," Lily said. "I love being around people, but sometimes I want to be left alone, too. Not very often, though, and definitely not out here in a storm." She shivered. "I've been in plenty of storms, but none that nearly killed me."

He grunted. "Should've been prepared."

Sparrow's spine stiffened. This was her first time back in the field in almost two years. She'd been so careful in making sure she did everything right, determined to prove she knew what she was doing and not let anyone get hurt on her watch again.

She raised her chin a notch. "We were as prepared as possible, under the circumstances. I didn't have many options when anticipating all possibilities. The storm wasn't forecasted, but I set up camp far enough away from that tall tree just in case the unexpected happened. The wind was fiercer than I've ever been in and blew the falling branch further than what I could imagine. The chances of this happening were slim."

"Yet it happened, and that's the point." His face

hardened. "You shouldn't be in the woods if you don't know how to survive." His gaze shot to Lily. "Especially when you have others depending on you."

Sparrow flinched. He was right. It had happened before. She couldn't let it happen again. Old demons started rising to the surface, threatening to choke her.

"Hey, we're not amateurs, and this isn't Sparrow's fault." Lily frowned at the man. "Geez, lighten up, Mister. No one could have predicted that branch to blow that far and land exactly on top of our tent," Lily continued. "Look, we appreciate the hospitality, but your *personality* could use some serious work."

Sparrow smiled her thanks to Lily and pushed her doubts and fears aside, refusing to lose herself again. She was strong and capable and good at her job. This was just a little setback, and they would get through it. They had to.

He cleared his throat, his forehead creasing. "Sorry. I'm not very good with people. It's getting late. You should get some sleep. When the weather clears, you should go back to your field work site and steer clear of this part of the woods."

"Why?" Sparrow asked, trying to figure this guy out. He didn't seem like a bad guy, but he didn't seem good, either. He seemed strange. There was a mystery surrounding him she couldn't quite figure out.

"Let's just say nothing good happens this deep into the woods." With that, he packed up his makeshift kitchen then lay down on his sleeping mat and rolled so he could face the opening of the cave, his gun a mere inch from his hand.

Sparrow and Lily looked at each other with raised eyebrows, but they didn't say another word. Their clothes had dried, so they got dressed and wrapped themselves back up in the thermal blankets that had been a godsend and lay down.

As soon as they were settled, he blew out the last candle.

Exhausted from the day's events, it wasn't long before Sparrow felt her entire body grow heavy. Lily had already drifted off to sleep, judging by her slowed breathing. Sparrow tried to fight it, not sure she wanted to sleep around this stranger, but she couldn't help it. Her eyes felt like sand was weighing them down until she could no longer keep them open. Giving up on fighting a losing battle, she drifted into a sleep deeper than any she could remember, with one last thought whispering through her brain...

What was in that medicinal tea?

* * *

THE NEXT MORNING, just as soon as it was dawn, Greyson headed out in his jeep with his assistant ranger, Willy Tucker. The storm had stopped in the middle of the night. Greyson had tried Sparrow's radio a couple more times, but she still didn't answer.

He was starting to get worried.

He had decided to investigate on his own before jumping the gun and calling search and rescue. The little bit he knew about Sparrow told him she would *not* appreciate being rescued. Better just him and his assistant than the cavalry. For once, Willy hadn't taken a day off or called in sick, even though his car had an oil leak just that morning. He was always tinkering with vehicles and stained with grease.

"Who are these people again?" Willy scrubbed a hand over his dirty blond buzzed hair. He was a big boy, tall and stocky, but not very bright.

"Wildlife biologists. They're doing field work on bird conservation."

"Then why are they so far inland?" Willy scratched his jaw.

"Fall migration. They're restoring the habitat and taking stock of which species are settling inland for the winter."

"Ah." Willy puckered his brow. "And why is it that they need us?"

Greyson sighed, beginning to wonder if bringing Willy along would be a help or a hindrance. "They might not, but as a ranger, it's my duty to make sure they're safe. They haven't answered their radio since the storm hit."

"Gotcha." The young man chewed his gum and popped a bubble as he looked out the window.

Greyson shook his head and focused on the road, trying to keep his irritation at bay. He knew the location of Sparrow's camp, so he drove down the logging road until he reached the switch point. Killing the engine to his jeep, he jogged over to her truck and looked in the window.

"Any luck?" Willy walked over to him at a much slower pace.

"No." Greyson softly cursed.

He had been hoping the women had been able to reach the truck and take shelter. Glancing around, he didn't see their ATVs either. He'd towed a couple of ATVs and packs filled with rescue materials just in case. Securing the packs onto the four-wheelers, he zipped up his coat and slipped on his gloves. Willy did the same, and with a nod, they fired up their engines and headed into the woods.

Greyson could see the women's tire tracks still, which told him they had made it to camp at least. He had to stay positive and focused. He traveled along the trail for what felt like hours when he knew it wasn't.

Finally, he came to the clearing where Sparrow had told him they had planned to set up camp.

So where was their tent?

He looked around, confused, until he spotted the massive tree branch which had fallen during the storm. His heart started pounding, and he began to sweat even though it was chilly out. There was no mistaking the material sticking out from beneath the branch.

The Maine Department of Conservation issued tent.

He cut the engine to his four-wheeler and ran over to the tent with Willy right behind him. "Sparrow? Lily? Can you hear me?"

Nothing.

"Oh, man, that doesn't look good. I can't imagine anyone surviving that." Willy walked around the tent, inspecting it.

"It's not our job to imagine anything. Let's clear the debris and see what we find." Greyson pulled a mini chainsaw from his pack and started cutting smaller branches off the big one.

Willy did the same on the other side.

When they had cleared enough branches out of the way, Greyson crawled under what he could. There were mounds beneath the material that made his mouth go dry. He prayed it wasn't human remains. Inhaling a deep breath, he drew on his training and stayed focused as he cut the tent open with a knife. Relief poured through him. The mounds were their packs and other supplies.

No humans in sight.

He stood. "All clear."

"Well, that's good," Willy wrinkled his forehead, "but where are they if all their stuff is here?"

Greyson's relief was short-lived.

The women had obviously escaped the falling tree,

but they would have had to take shelter. "They wouldn't have risked taking the ATVs all the way back to the truck during a thunderstorm, for fear of a lightning strike. They must have gone off on foot to look for shelter."

Willy's eyes widened. "Deeper into the woods?"

"That's my best guess." Wandering around the tent, Greyson looked for clues. He noticed a trace of deep footprints left from the mud. Kneeling down to inspect them, dread filled him. "These footprints are way too large to be either Sparrow's or Lily's."

"You think other biologists were here?"

"None were scheduled." Greyson narrowed his eyebrows as he looked at Willy. "It's either a private group, or someone who shouldn't be here."

"Poachers?" Willy asked with a worried tone.

Greyson set his jaw and said through his teeth, "Maybe."

"Maybe we should go back for reinforcements."

"Reinforcements we don't have."

"Poachers are dangerous people, boss." Willy paced. "Not people you want to mess around with."

"I understand that, but I'm not leaving these women alone any longer than I have to. Are you with me, or not, Willy?"

Willy only hesitated a moment before nodding. "What do you want to do, boss?"

Greyson kept searching until he found footprints that looked small enough to be the women. "Track them."

"In there?" Willy paced some more. "But that's a remote section of woods where no one goes. I doubt they went that way."

"That's the way their tracks go, and so do we." Greyson stared hard at Willy. "Are you up to this job or not?"

Willy hesitated again, then nodded and grabbed his pack.

"Good. We can't afford to waste any more time. Follow me." Greyson grabbed his own pack and headed into the woods after the footprints.

They traveled quite a ways, with Willy on edge still, looking around constantly. Greyson couldn't blame him. It was the rut for deer and moose. Not to mention bears and bobcats were around. Mating season could be dangerous, and with poachers on the loose as well, they had to stay alert.

Finally, the tracks stopped outside a cave.

"There." Greyson pointed to the cave up a slight hill.

Willy nodded and took up the rear as Greyson led the way in front. They both drew their weapons as they neared the opening. There had once been a fire made at the opening, which led Greyson to believe no animals were inside. But that didn't mean there wasn't a threat.

"Stay out here and keep watch while I go inside and check it out," he said to Willy.

"Roger that." Willy planted his feet and faced out.

Greyson drew his weapon and slowly crept inside, not calling out either of the women's names in case they weren't alone. He reached a bend and the path opened into a large area. He nearly dropped to his knees.

Sparrow lay curled in a ball on the floor beneath a thermal blanket.

Sheathing his weapon, he ran to her and gently knelt down. He felt the pulse in her neck just to be sure. Strong and steady. Thank the Lord, his little songbird was alive. His lips tipped up slightly at the corners. She was softly snoring, still fast asleep.

He brushed his fingertips over her cheek. "Sparrow, wake up."

She moaned and snuggled deeper beneath her

blanket until nothing but her silky burgundy hair stuck out the top.

He chuckled, pulling the edge of the blanket down. "Come on, sleeping beauty, it's time to get up."

"Five more minutes," she said groggily.

"It's already well past dawn. Time to get up."

Her movements stilled. "It is?" she asked sleepily, opening confused pale gray eyes. "I never sleep in." She slowly sat up and looked around. "Where am I?"

"You're in a cave, deep in the woods." He looked her over. "Are you hurt? Did you hit your head?"

She ran a hand over her scalp and shook her head, then winced. "No, but I have a whopper of a headache. If I didn't know better, I would swear I have a hangover. But that's not possible. I don't drink anymore."

He drew his brows together. "Do you remember anything?"

"Yeah, Lily and I had to make a run for it after lightning hit a tree and it fell on our tent. We got out just in time."

"I saw. Anything else you remember?"

"We headed into the woods and found a cave, but we weren't alone."

He frowned, glancing around. "Who was here?"

"I don't know his name. Some guy with long hair and a long beard. He was dressed all in camo and had a pack filled with survival stuff. He gave us blankets and venison and tea." She glanced around. "Everything is gone. He must have split before we woke up."

Greyson narrowed his eyes. "What kind of tea?"

She shrugged. "I don't know. He called it medicinal tea. It tasted earthy to me, but I was freezing so I drank it. Lily said she didn't like tea, so she only had water." Sparrow puckered her brow. "I think he put something in it. I feel like I've been drugged." She looked around at the empty cave. "Where's Lily?"

"I was going to ask you the same thing."

He saw the moment his words sank in. "Ohmigod, she's not here?" Sparrow scrambled to her feet. "Her blanket is gone, she's gone, he's gone, his supplies are gone, everything is gone. I knew there was something off about him. I think he took her." She wrung her hands and paced. "We have to find her. I can't let anyone else go missing, too."

He stood and settled his hands on her shoulders to stop her. "Hey, easy now. You're not going to do anyone any good by falling apart. I'm here now, and I'm not going anywhere. Okay?" He waited until her eyes locked onto his and focused. "That's good. Deep breaths, in and out slowly. Let's retrace your steps and see what we can find."

He wasn't going to promise her that everything would be okay because it might not be. Too many people had said the same thing to him, filling him with hope. False hope. He'd learned that the hard way and wasn't about to put anyone else through that, but he also wasn't about to stop looking.

He didn't like the thought of some maniac running around in his woods.

7

LILY WOKE UP, dazed and confused. She couldn't see anything. She tried to move her hands to her eyes, but they were bound together behind her back. Her legs were bound, too. She felt material tied around her eyes and a rag in her mouth.

She was freezing.

She sat on something hard. Leaning back until her fingertips skimmed beneath her butt, she realized she was on a floor of some kind. There wasn't any heat, but she could hear the wind whipping outside.

So she was indoors, but where?

The woods had sugar shanties and hunting cabins. Maybe whoever had taken her had put her in one of those? But why? There were also plenty of warehouses in town. She could be anywhere. At least she took comfort in knowing she wasn't in a cave or outside where a wild animal could get her.

That would be a horrible way to die.

Struggling to remember what had happened, she concentrated hard. Her head ached something fierce, and then everything came back to her. She had fallen right to sleep at first, then woke up and tossed and turned most of the night on the hard floor of the cave until sleep finally claimed her once more. When she woke up a second time, Sparrow was sound asleep, softly snoring.

The wild man was gone, along with all his supplies.

Lily remembered being happy about that because he'd left them alive. Fear consumed her now. She had ventured outside to find a place in the woods to go to the bathroom. When she was finished, she was about to head back to the cave when she heard voices.

Creeping ahead to investigate, she saw a group of men she'd never seen before, standing there talking intensely. They had weapons, but they didn't seem like a group of hunters. She couldn't hear what they were saying, but she thought she detected a foreign accent. A bird squawked overhead, and she jumped, rustling the underbrush around her.

All eyes turned in her direction, so she ducked lower.

She heard them take a few steps towards her hiding place. She smelled a scent she'd smelled before—a chemical type of smell mixed—but couldn't quite place it seconds before she felt the presence of someone behind her. She tried to turn around, but something hard hit her head and she blacked out.

All she knew for certain was that she had been taken.

* * *

GREYSON, Sparrow, and Willy searched the woods for over an hour to no avail. There was no sign of any wild man in the woods or Lily or anyone else, for that matter. Greyson had convinced her to go with him back to The Cove and report Lily missing to the sheriff and chief of police.

Sparrow was distraught and still a little groggy, but

she'd finally agreed to leave the woods…for now…but only to go straight to the sheriff's office. She refused to see a doctor. Said she wasn't about to waste time on herself when Lily was still out there.

Greyson had instructed Willy to drive the forestry jeep with the ATVs back to the office, while Greyson drove Sparrow's conservation truck. They'd gathered her pack but left Lily's pack, the two-way radio, and her ATVs at the tent in case she returned there.

Pulling into the parking lot of the large building where the sheriff's office, the police station, the crime lab, and the medical examiner were located, Greyson cut the engine to the truck. He paused a beat, not wanting to rush Sparrow.

"You ready?" he finally asked her.

She looked like she'd weathered a storm with wrinkled clothes, tangled hair, and smudges on her cheeks. She squeezed her eyes tight for a moment, and then opened them with determination and nodded.

"Yes. Every second counts."

"Agreed."

He climbed out, and she joined him as they walked in the sunshine across the parking lot. What a difference a day made in this neck of the woods. Making their way inside the building, they stopped into the sheriff's office after hearing Trent and Hank's voices. The men looked up at them in surprise.

"What happened to you?" Trent eyed Sparrow with raised brows.

"We got caught in the storm." She stared at a picture of Trent, Stacy, and baby Lizzie, then looked away and wrapped her arms around her middle before continuing. "Lightning hit a tree, and it came crashing down on our tent."

"Was anyone hurt?" Hank asked.

Sparrow's lips trembled. "We found shelter in a cave

after nearly succumbing to hypothermia, but th-this morning…Lily went missing."

Trent frowned. "What do you mean, she went missing?"

"There was a wild man." Sparrow started pacing as she rambled. "He gave us thermal blankets and venison and some weird medicinal tea. Although, Lily doesn't like tea, so she had water. I was the only one who drank the tea, and I slept like the dead."

"It's true. She was out cold when Willy and I showed up," Greyson added.

Sparrow nodded. "I was groggy and disoriented when Greyson woke me up. The cave was empty. The wild man, his supplies, and Lily were all gone."

"Wild man? Are you sure you weren't hallucinating from the hypothermia?" Hank asked, raising an eyebrow at Trent and Greyson.

"What did this man look like?" Trent studied her closely.

"He wore camo clothing and had long hair with a long beard. He had lots of supplies and seemed to know his way around the woods." She looked at them with a desperate expression on her face. "I know I sound crazy, but I promise you I'm not. I know what I saw. He wouldn't tell us why he was in the woods. He just said he wanted to be left alone. And he warned us about the woods being dangerous." She wrung her hands together. "I think he took Lily. She wouldn't have wandered off on her own."

"We searched the area, but her footprints literally disappeared," Greyson said. "As if she vanished."

"Or maybe someone took her on an ATV," Hank said.

Sparrow stared off as if remembering. "Maybe it wasn't the wild man. Maybe it was the other wildlife biologists we ran in to."

Trent's forehead creased. "Other biologists?"

"Yes, they were in our spot when we arrived. They said they worked for a private lab called Conservation Consultants."

"That far inland?" Hank's brow wrinkled. "Don't private labs usually work with various companies who want to make sure their products and practices are environmentally friendly? Why on earth would they need to check on the environment that far inland instead of just around their businesses?"

"Exactly," Sparrow said. "And they didn't have clearance to work on that site. I told them they were interfering with the state's work. The man said there must have been a miscommunication somewhere. Then he warned us about the woods being dangerous, same as the wild man did. I didn't trust the wild man, and I trusted these men even less. All I know is Lily wouldn't have gone off in the woods alone, and she wouldn't have gotten lost."

"Do you have any names we can look into?" Hank pulled out a notebook and pen from his jacket.

"They said their names were Ozzy Price and Peter LaCroix." Sparrow rubbed her arms as Hank jotted down notes.

"I hate to say it, but what about the possibility of a wild animal attack?" Trent looked at Greyson who was already shaking his head.

"We would have seen evidence of a struggle," he glanced at Sparrow, "or a dismembered body."

She shuddered, her face turning pale.

"But we didn't, so I'm sure that's not the case," he quickly added.

"We have to do something," she said in barely more than a whisper. "I can't handle someone else going missing because of me," she muttered more to herself.

"We'll organize a broader search." Trent pulled out a map.

"I'll touch base with both of our departments as well as a call for volunteers, and we'll start first thing tomorrow morning." Hank wrote down more notes.

"Tomorrow?" Sparrow stopped pacing. "But what about today?"

"Willy and I already searched a good portion of the woods between the cave and the field work site but didn't find anything," Greyson said. "By the time Trent and Hank organize a search party, we'll lose what remaining sunlight we have left. We don't want anyone out in those woods at night."

"But Lily's all alone out there." Sparrow's voice hitched. "She can't handle another night alone."

"Look, I've known Lily longer than you have." Greyson rested his hands on Sparrow's shoulders until she looked at him. "She's tough. If someone has her, they'll keep her alive until they voice their demands. And if she's alone, she'll find her way back to your tent where she has her pack and supplies. She knows what to do."

"What if she thinks I abandoned her?" The look on Sparrow's face told him this was about a lot more than Lily.

"People who have met you know you wouldn't do that. You're not going to be any good to anyone if you don't go home and get some rest." He dropped his hands and let them hang at his sides before he did something stupid like pull her in for a hug. It still amazed him he could feel this strongly about someone so quickly. All he wanted to do was hold her. Comfort her.

Kiss her.

"He's right," Trent said.

Trent's words snapped Greyson back to reality, and

he tore his gaze away from Sparrow's lips. He could feel her looking at him with puzzled eyes.

"We can call one of your friends to stay with you if you want," Hank added, pulling her attention away from Greyson.

Greyson inhaled a deep breath of relief. She'd just been through trauma, and here he was thinking about kissing her. The last thing he needed to do was scare her away.

"Thank you all, but I'm fine. I think I'll just go back to my hotel and call it a day." Sparrow stood.

"I'll drive you," Greyson said.

"Actually, I think I'm going to walk. I need to clear my head, and my hotel is just down the street."

"Are you sure?" Greyson didn't like the thought of her walking by herself, but he couldn't think of anything to make her listen to reason.

"I'm sure. Thanks for all your help, but I'd like to be alone now." She waved to them all and headed out the door.

Greyson stood there, feeling helpless, but he couldn't do a damn thing about it. Yet something told him she wasn't out of danger just yet.

Well, hell.

* * *

SPARROW'S PHONE rang while she walked down the street toward her hotel. She checked the caller ID and groaned, contemplating not answering. She wanted to shut the world out and ignore her problems, but she wasn't the same person as before. She was stronger now.

This time she had the tools to cope with a crisis.

"Hi, Victoria," she finally answered.

Sparrow had wanted to live in a small town after all

the turmoil a big city had brought her, but small-town life was different. Nobody had secrets and news spread faster than a wildfire. She had anticipated this call but had thought she might at least get one day's reprieve.

"Sparrow, thank goodness you're all right," Victoria said through the phone, her voice sounding frantic. "Chris and I have been worried sick about you."

"I'm okay. I was going to call you. I just needed a minute."

"That's totally understandable. I would have waited until tomorrow to call, but I just needed to hear your voice and have you tell me directly that you're okay. I haven't slept a wink since the storm rolled in and have been checking in on all my teams. You were the only team I couldn't get through to. How's Lily?"

A pause filled the line. "She's missing."

"What?"

Sparrow sighed, then filled her boss in on everything that had happened. "The sheriff and chief are organizing a search party for tomorrow morning. I'm not happy about that. I'd like to go back out there today."

"You shouldn't be going anywhere except the hospital to get checked out. I know you're in a good place now, Sparrow, but don't slack off on taking care of yourself."

"I'm okay. I promise. Nothing a hot shower and a hot meal won't fix." Sparrow refused to think about the bottle of liquor she had bought to test herself, relieved she had emptied it. Now was not the time to be testing herself, but she felt like if she got through this, she could get through anything.

"What happened out there, Sparrow?" Victoria spoke in a sympathetic voice, but Sparrow could hear the confusion. She couldn't blame her. She was confused herself.

"I honestly don't know. I checked the weather and

planned for the unexpected, but that lightning strike was a fluke. I promise you, I put our tent in the best possible location given the circumstances."

"Maybe you weren't quite ready to go back in the field. That's my fault. I shouldn't have pushed you. I should have eased you back into it."

That stung. Sparrow knew how to do her job and was damned good at it. One poor lapse in judgment in the past had cost her so much. She refused to let that happen again. "I'm ready. I swear I am. I need this job. Please don't give up on me, Victoria."

"I'm not going to give up on you, hon. I'm just thinking of your well-being and giving you space until you're ready."

"I'm ready. I'm getting back out in the field just as soon as I can, and I won't stop looking until Lily is found."

"Please let the police handle this, Sparrow. I don't need two of my people in jeopardy. Your field project can wait."

"Of course. I'll keep you posted if I hear anything more." Sparrow hung up, having no intention of sitting back and doing nothing to help. She couldn't stop blaming herself for what had happened.

She walked further down Main Street, taking deep breaths and trying to refocus. Her nerves finally calmed down, when suddenly, a strong feeling that she was being watched swept over her. Her blood pressure spiked once more. She spun around in a circle but didn't see anything. Paranoia held her frozen in its clutches for a moment, but she fell back on her therapy sessions and started deep breathing once more. She blinked. How had she ended up here? She looked up at the sign above the store she stood in front of.

Harbor Spirits Liquor Store.

She couldn't fall back into her old ways of coping.

Closing her eyes, she took a few more deep breaths. When she opened her eyes again, she gasped. Whipping around, she looked behind her and nearly ran into the hunter from the Lost Horizon.

"Whoa, there, young lady." He steadied her. "Not again." He chuckled as recognition dawned in his eyes. "Name's Abe. I figured if we keep bumping into each other, we might as well meet officially." He held out his hand.

"Sparrow." She shook his hand and laughed, happy for the distraction. "Any more luck with your hunting season?"

"Nah, but there's still time. I'm bound to get lucky one of these days." He opened the door to the liquor store and held it open. "Ladies first."

She took a step back. "Oh, no thanks. I'm not going in. I was just window shopping, but I'm all set."

"Suit yourself." He gave her a wave and then went inside the store.

Sparrow let out a big sigh. She could have sworn she'd seen Harlow's reflection in the store's window. Her heartbeat, which had hammered in her ears, faded away. This whole ordeal was simply bringing up the past, she rationalized. It had to be.

You're not crazy, she told herself.

Continuing down the street, she still felt eyes on the back of her, but she refused to let herself fall victim to old ghosts. She didn't turn around and didn't stop walking until she reached Coldwater Commons. Making her way inside, she nodded to the front desk clerk, then walked down the hall until she reached her hotel room door.

Sparrow let herself inside, then closed and locked the door firmly behind her. Taking a moment to lean back against the door and close her eyes, she finally processed all that had transpired in the past twenty-four hours.

Her brain relived every moment, second guessing if there was something she could have done differently. She honestly didn't think there was. She'd followed her training and had done everything in her power to keep them safe. There was something in that tea. There had to have been because she'd slept like the dead and hadn't heard a single thing.

Coldwater Cove was not turning out to be the fresh start she'd anticipated.

The other biologists clearly hadn't wanted her intruding on whatever studies they were conducting, yet when she and Lily had taken their samples, they hadn't found evidence of studies of *any* kind being conducted. It didn't make sense. And that wild man had looked like something right out of a movie. He'd confused her. Why would he help them only to drug her?

Where was Lily?

Every time Sparrow thought about it, she felt herself sliding towards a nervous breakdown. Could the biologists have kidnapped Lily? They had headed off from the field site in the opposite direction she and Lily had come from. So where had they gone? And then the wild man had vanished without a trace, as if he'd never existed.

Did he take her?

She hadn't seen an ATV out there, yet Lily's footsteps disappeared shortly beyond the cave. Did she wander outside to go to the bathroom or something and an animal got her? Greyson had said there were no signs of a struggle and no animal prints.

None of it made sense.

Tears threatened to overtake her. Exhaustion finally won out, making her muscles weak. Her entire body ached. She walked like a zombie to the bathroom, turned the shower on hot, then stripped off her clothes and stepped inside the steaming spray.

Greyson's face appeared before her mind's eye.

She might be a bit rusty, but she'd been around long enough to know when a man was interested in her. He was so handsome, and honestly, he was the first man she'd even thought about in that way since her fiancé had gone missing almost two years ago. The problem was, she didn't have closure. If she knew whether he was alive or dead, then maybe she could move on.

But she might never know, and that was a reality she needed to accept.

Turning the water off, she wrapped herself in a towel and went to find something warm to snuggle up in. She planned to sleep for a few hours, get something to eat at The Claw for dinner, and then see what she could find out about the search party plans for tomorrow.

Heading into the bedroom part of her suite, she opened her dresser drawer to pull out some clothes and stopped short. She was meticulous in how she put her things away. To the average person, things might look completely normal.

Not to her.

One of her shirts was folded just a hair differently than she would normally do. Even as frazzled as she had been lately, she still wouldn't have strayed from her normal organized routine, making one thing crystal clear...

Someone had been in her room.

8

"Dammit! It's not my fault," I grumbled to myself the next morning.

I kept to the shadows at the edge of the crowd. They'd been gathering by the state offices next to the woods for the past hour to form a search party for the missing wildlife biology assistant. If stupid Lily and Sparrow had just stayed at their field site, then none of this would have happened.

They were warned the woods could be dangerous.

I'd had no choice but to take Lily. The stupid woman had drawn the attention of men who would be all too happy to kill her. I'd had to knock her out so they wouldn't see her and then leave her there as I rushed forward so they would think I was the one who had made the noise.

She should be thanking me.

Luckily, she remained passed out long enough for me to go back for her. Fucking storm ruined everything. I never expected to run into them that far into the woods. I was always careful and disguised myself for this very reason.

I couldn't let anyone in town learn about my secret.

I looked toward the group of people and narrowed

my eyes. Sparrow was front and center—right up by the mayor, sheriff, and chief of police—alongside that forest ranger, Greyson Adler. He made me nervous with his survival skills and how often he went deep into the woods. He seemed to go above and beyond the call of his ranger duties.

Why?

And now he and Sparrow looked like they were getting awfully chummy, and that didn't sit well with me. The last thing I needed was for him to guide her into venturing even further into parts unknown. They wouldn't find what they were looking for.

I'd hidden Lily well.

But they just might find something else they had no business knowing about. I couldn't let that happen. I'd gotten in too deep to the point where there was no way out for me, and I wasn't about to go down without a fight.

Shit.

It looked like the search party was about to start. I needed to put my game face on and join in. At least that way I could control where the parties searched. I would simply make sure I was assigned to the area I didn't want anyone else looking. I wasn't an evil person by nature, and my stomach churned with the thought of what I might have to do. I ground my teeth until my jaw ached. I didn't want to hurt anyone, but I would if I had to.

And it would all be Sparrow James' fault.

* * *

"Does everyone know where they are going to search?" Trent asked the crowd before him with Stacy by his side.

"And does anyone need a map?" Hank took a stack of papers from Olivia and held them up before him.

"Make sure you all have a reliable way of communicating," Laura added, pointing to her husband.

Tommy demonstrated by holding up a walkie talkie and two-way radio. "Especially those of you covering areas further inland. The cell reception out there is spotty at best, so you'll need something better."

Greyson looked around, impressed with the turnout.

Tia Johnson and her brothers had closed their real estate office so their entire staff could be there. Kimberly Caldwell and the rest of the town council, as well as Mark Jessup and the rest of the school board, all put aside their differences and were volunteering to search as well. Jack and the rest of his staff closed The Claw to help out, and so did Betty Clark from The Lost Horizon. Even the maintenance man, Larry, and his assistant, Buck, were there to help search. Anyone who met Lily, even strangers, loved her.

Greggor and Nigel had even put aside their differences to rise to the occasion.

Pretty much the entire town, other than the harbormaster, had shut down to assist. Zoe couldn't leave the harbor unattended, but she let her staff join the search party. Coldwater Cove looked out for their own. When one of them needed something, everyone showed up to lend their support. Even strangers in town for hunting and the fall activities took time out to help with the search and rescue operation.

Just one more reason why Greyson had never left his hometown.

Sparrow might be new, but Lily had lived here all her life as well. He'd hated that the days were so short now. The thought of her out there on her own overnight had killed him, but he couldn't risk losing anyone else in the dark.

Trent and Hank had both agreed.

Greyson had to believe Lily would be savvy enough to fall back on her survival skills. The frost could be deadly this time of year. If she got hurt or was unconscious, she could freeze to death overnight. And if she wasn't alone, she knew self-defense.

He'd made sure all the departments of each of the departments were capable of basic survival skills and self-defense moves, especially after his mother had gone missing five years ago. He still had nightmares over what she may have gone through…or was still going through.

And then there was Sparrow.

He glanced at her. She was dressed in proper field attire for the weather and knew what she was doing in the wild, but she was so damn small. He knew her well enough now to know she would hate it if she knew he felt that way.

She had her walls up, so it was hard to know what she'd been through. He suspected she'd been through a lot in her past. And Coldwater Cove hadn't treated her well so far. He intended to change that if she would let him.

"Greyson, I said are you ready to go?" Sparrow gave him a strange look. "Are you okay? You seem a million miles away."

He blinked. "Yeah, I was just thinking."

"Everyone's heading out. Can you walk and think at the same time? I really want to get going." She looked up at him with tired eyes and a slight droop to her shoulders. If he had to guess, he'd bet she hadn't slept a wink.

"Roger that." He frowned as they started walking. "I

should be asking you if you're okay. You look exhausted."

"I didn't sleep last night." She stared straight ahead as she walked.

"I wondered why you didn't go to The Claw for dinner last night. I thought you must have been worn out and slept through dinner."

"Nope, I ordered in. Too stressed out to go anywhere."

"How come? Because you're worried about Lily?"

She paused a beat. "That, and I think someone was in my hotel room yesterday."

He stopped short and grabbed her arm. "Wait, what was that?"

"I'll explain on the way." She took his hand and pulled him along until they reached his jeep.

Everyone was driving down the logging trail and then heading off in all directions from there on foot until they covered a manageable area of where Lily could have possibly gone. Once they were on their way, Sparrow started talking.

"I know what you're going to say. I should have called the police."

"Or me."

She rubbed her temples then tucked a burgundy strand of hair behind her ear. "I was still groggy from whatever was in that tea, so I thought maybe I had imagined it. I knew you all had more important things to worry about, like finding Lily."

"Your safety is just as important, but I'll play devil's advocate. What makes you think you didn't imagine it."

"I know myself. I'm extremely organized when it comes to my personal property. Even when I was a mess personally, my material things were still meticulous. The average person probably wouldn't have noticed anything off, but when I went to get dressed after my shower yesterday, my clothing was slightly crooked in my drawers."

"Was your door locked?"

"Yes. I have no idea how someone got in. And it wasn't like a normal tossing of someone's room when a thief is looking for something. This was more disturbing. It was subtle. Like someone had gone through my things very carefully, obviously not wanting me to know they were there...or knowingly messing with my head."

"Was anything missing?"

"No. That was another reason why I didn't call the police. I didn't really have anything to report, other than my suspicions. Still, it freaks me out staying there alone now. How did the person get in? What if they come back?"

Greyson was already shaking his head. "I don't think you should stay there alone, either. Too many questionable things have been going on lately. I live in the house I grew up in on the water if you want to stay with me."

"I don't think that's—"

He held up his hand to cut her off. "Look, I'm offering this as a friend. At least until Tia finds you something more permanent. No strings attached; I promise." Even though he felt more and more drawn to her every day, he knew she wasn't ready for that. "I'm an only child. The house has three bedrooms and two bathrooms. You could have your own space, and frankly, it would be nice to have some company."

She hesitated for so long, he didn't think she was going to respond. Finally, she nodded almost as if to herself. "Okay, I'll do it. And thank you. I can admit that I would feel better not being alone right now."

"Good, then it's settled."

"Oh, look, we're here." She pointed at the turn off

where people left their vehicles to venture forth on ATVs or foot. Her mouth twisted into a frown, and she squinted. "What are *they* doing here?"

Greyson's gaze followed hers to two men he didn't recognize, standing by their own truck, ATVs, and supplies. "Who are they?"

"The other wildlife biologists I met in the woods that I told you guys about. When they left our field site, they took off in the other direction. I have no idea what they're doing at this location again. I didn't see them in town during the search party organization. If they had been, then they would know we were all assigned different locations."

Greyson cut the engine to his jeep. "Stay here while I—"

"Not a chance." Sparrow was already halfway out of the jeep before he had even put his hand on his door handle.

He yanked his door open and slid out of the driver's side, double-checking to make sure he had his concealed carry hidden beneath his coat. He always wore it but was finding a need to more than ever these days. "Wait for me at least." His long strides caught him up to her short legs quickly.

The woman was going to be the death of him yet.

"What are you doing here?" Sparrow asked, folding her arms over her chest, and glaring at the men.

"News travels fast around these parts." The tall thin redhead adjusted his glasses on his nose. "We had just set up another field site when that doozy of a thunderstorm hit. We rode it out in our tent, then went back to check on you two. We've always been about helping fellow comrades in the field no matter who they work for." He looked her in the eye. "Wouldn't you do the same?"

"Of course," she studied them suspiciously, "but you didn't stick around very long to try to find us."

"Your tent was demolished," the shorter, stocky dark one said. "We didn't see anyone inside, so we assumed you wandered off. Frankly, we didn't think either of you survived in that kind of weather."

"It wasn't until we made it into town that we heard about you getting rescued and your friend going missing," the first one added. "We restocked our supplies but figured we would try to help before heading back to our own site."

"I'm Ranger Adler." Greyson stepped forward between Sparrow and them as he held out his hand. "And you are…?"

"Sorry," Sparrow interjected, shaking off her frustration and inhaling a deep breath as she took her place beside him. "Greyson, this is wildlife biologist Ozzy Price and his assistant, Peter LaCroix."

"Nice to meet you, Ranger." Ozzy shook his hand and smiled pleasantly. He seemed harmless enough, but Sparrow didn't seem to trust him. That was enough to make Greyson keep his guard up.

"Good to meet you as well, Mr. Price." Greyson shook his hand and then held his palm out to the other man. "Mr. LaCroix?"

A muscle in Peter's jaw twitched and he only hesitated a moment before nodding once and shaking Greyson's hand. "At your service, Ranger."

"Actually, we have this area covered." Greyson studied them both.

"If you had stayed for the search party briefing," Sparrow pointed out, "you would have known that everyone was assigned a certain area so we wouldn't waste time covering the same place."

"My bad." Ozzy tilted his head and saluted Sparrow. "We're only trying to help, Ms. James."

Sparrow hesitated, then relaxed slightly. "Well, thank you for that. Sorry for being a bit suspicious. I just want to find my partner. We could use all the help we can get."

"Understood. We would be the same way." Ozzy glanced at Peter, and the man nodded his agreement.

"Why don't you gentlemen head to your new field site, proving you got the proper permission this time. You can bet I will be following up on that, but right now, finding Lily is top priority," Greyson interjected. "If you see anything, use your two-way radio to report in."

"You got it." Ozzy saluted Greyson then bowed his head to Sparrow. "Good luck out there."

She nodded her thanks.

Peter followed behind Ozzy, and Greyson could have sworn his eyes narrowed when he passed Sparrow. Ozzy might seem harmless enough, but there was something about Peter that Greyson didn't like. He had an edge to him like no other biology assistant Greyson had ever met. Who was he?

And what exactly was he doing in Greyson's woods?

* * *

"ANY WORD?" Trent radioed Hank.

All the parties had been searching for hours to no avail. The sun was setting, and the temperature was dropping. They couldn't stay out there much longer, or they would be putting more lives at stake.

"None," Hank replied. "We've got about an hour left of daylight and those trails are dangerous without adequate light. Some of these volunteers don't have enough experience. I think we should call it."

"Agreed. You contact your half of the groups, and I'll

handle mine. We can pick up where we left off at dawn."

"I'm on it."

Trent hung up. Stacy had already left to feed Lizzie, and Laura had gone with her to pick up her girls. Olivia was still with Hank, and Tommy had stayed with Trent, still searching about twenty feet away. Greyson and Sparrow had gone radio silent. Trent would normally be worried about that, but Greyson knew more about survival than almost anyone he'd ever met.

Trent's radio buzzed with static, which always happened just before someone spoke. He lifted it to his ear and listened.

"I found something," came a voice Trent knew well but never expected to hear over his field radio.

Trent looked up to make sure Tommy was far enough away not to overhear them. "What are you doing calling me on the two-way radio? The deal is I call you in case someone is with me. Anyone could have heard you."

"I couldn't wait, and there's no cell service out here. I had no choice."

Trent scrubbed a hand over the back of his neck. He'd been working with this informant for a while now, but no one knew. He couldn't risk blowing everything he'd worked so hard for. Setting his jaw, he muttered, "In the future, do me a favor. Try to find another more private way to reach me."

"Do you want to hear what I found our not?"

Trent sighed. "Are you alone."

"Yes."

Giving one more glance in Tommy's direction, Trent turned the volume down a little and responded, "Let's hear it, then."

"Her pack is gone."

His forehead wrinkled. "Come again?"

"Lily's pack. The girl didn't have it when she went missing. Her partner left it at their tent in case the girl came back for it. Now, it's missing. Either Lily came back for it, or someone else took it."

Trent clenched his jaw. He knew everyone who was in the woods at the moment and didn't think any of them would take Lily's pack without reporting it. That left the question, who was in the woods that he *didn't* know about...and why?

"Keep your eyes peeled and report back to me if you find anything else."

"Will do, but don't get mad if it's over your radio."

"Fine, but don't start talking right away. Say something like test first. Then if someone's there, I can make an excuse and step away. Can you at least do that for me?"

"Done. Gotta go. Someone's coming." The radio went back to static.

Trent disconnected just before Tommy reached his side.

"Who was that?" Tommy asked. "Did someone find something?"

Trent shook his head. "It was Hank."

Tommy gave him a funny look. "How can that be? I was literally just on the radio with him."

Dammit. "I mean, I talked to Hank a few moments ago. We decided to call it for today. I was contacting all the search parties to let them know. I still have more to do. I could use your help."

Tommy still looked at him a little suspiciously as he said, "Sure thing. Whatever you need."

Trent wanted to keep Tommy engaged. Lately, he had been acting more like himself and showing more of an interest in being part of their group than he had in a long time. Trent was hopeful that maybe Tommy and Laura were starting to work things out between them.

"Great. If you would continue making calls, that would be helpful."

"You got it." Tommy stepped away, making calls over his radio.

Trent packed up their gear while Tommy made calls. He hated being secretive with his friends. He hadn't even told Stacy everything because he didn't want to put anyone he cared about in danger. He was close to getting everything he was looking for. There was too much riding on the line, so for now, he was keeping silent.

If everything unfolded according to plan, it would all be worth it.

9

"WELL, THAT'S EVERYTHING." Sparrow closed the trunk to her car and walked inside Greyson's huge colonial that sat right on the ocean.

He'd said he had a house, but this looked more like a mansion to her. She'd grown up far differently than he had, obviously. He'd said his parents were both gone. His mom went missing, and his dad had left town. They'd either done very well for themselves in their career choices, or one of their families came from money. She was betting on the latter because she knew first-hand that working for the state didn't pay much.

"You certainly travel light." He followed her into the house and set her last bag on the massive island in the kitchen.

"I've never needed much to make me happy." She walked outside onto the back patio and stared out over the ocean.

Greyson had given her a tour when she'd first arrived before they'd carried her belongings inside. When you walked through the front door of Greyson's house, you passed a formal living room on one side and a family room on the other side of a staircase leading up to the guest bedrooms and bathroom. Past the stairs on the main floor, there was a master bedroom and bathroom. On the other side was a half bath followed by a large kitchen that opened into a morning room, facing the ocean, with a patio and chairs outside.

Walking to the edge of the patio, she noticed there was a path that led straight down a slight slope to the ocean. It reminded her of her father and her past. Taking a deep breath of crisp salty air, she felt like she could finally breathe.

Funny, she couldn't remember the last time she'd felt that way.

Greyson joined her several moments later and handed her a cup of steaming hot tea, content with the silence between them. After spending all day together in the woods, searching for Lily, she'd discovered a lot about him. He was a good listener, patient, kind, understanding, and supportive.

Whatever she had needed, he had given her.

"Thank you." She took the cup from him. "And thank you for letting me stay with you temporarily. I don't think I could be alone right now."

"You don't have to be alone." He sipped his strong black coffee and stared out at the sun sinking below the horizon. "I don't think anyone willingly chooses to be alone."

"I didn't either until we ran into that wild man." She shivered. "I just can't believe Lily has to spend another night alone in the woods, or wherever she is." She lifted her gaze up to his. "Why can't we find her?"

"Because she's not lost." Greyson glanced down at her with a serious expression. "I think someone took her."

He wasn't telling her something she wanted to hear, but Sparrow loved that he was direct with her. He didn't sugarcoat things and give her false hope. So many people had done that to her in the past. She would much rather have the truth, so she would know what she was facing.

It was easier to cope with the truth when you saw it coming.

She let out a shaky breath. "I think you're right. I hate that we have to stop looking before dark each day, especially when that happens so early this time of year. What else can we do?"

"We could start talking to people Lily knew in town. Find out if she had any enemies. Someone who might want to do her harm."

"Or maybe she didn't have any enemies, and this is someone she *didn't* know, who was already out in the woods. According to those maps you gave me, that cave we took shelter in is one of thousands in those woods. She could be anywhere."

"Not only that, but she could also be across the Canadian border already." He shook his head, still staring out over the water. "Unfortunately, people are killed or taken for all sorts of reasons around these parts."

"Oh, God, I hadn't thought of that." Sparrow grabbed Greyson's muscular arm, needing his strength. "You don't think she's been trafficked, do you?"

"Let's not get ahead of ourselves." He covered her hand with his own. "We can't afford to *think* anything. Been there, done that, and it's a slippery slope. We have to follow the facts and keep looking, or we'll go crazy imagining the worst."

Sparrow nodded and slid her hand out from beneath his. She was quickly becoming dependent on him, and she couldn't afford to be dependent on anyone. "You're right." She tried for a smile. "I need a distraction. Tell me about your family. How in the world did you grow up in a place like this?"

"Ah, the cottage." His lips twisted.

"Cottage?" She gaped at him. "This is no cottage."

"To my mother's family it is. She came from old money and grew up in a house about five times the size of this one."

Well, that explained a lot. "What about your father?"

"And therein lies the problem. He most definitely did *not* come from money. He was a ranger like me. My mother fell madly in love with him. Her parents forbade her to marry him, but she went against their wishes and did so anyway."

"Wow, I like her already." Sparrow couldn't stop grinning.

He chuckled. "She was really something. You remind me of her. Fiercely determined and headstrong."

She shrugged. "You have to be in my line of work."

"You have to be to survive in her family, as well." He sighed.

Sparrow's heart ached for him. "What happened?"

"She didn't care if they cut her off. Her happiness came first. As an only child like me, I think she knew they wouldn't disown her. They never accepted him, but when I came along, things were finally peaceful between them."

"Is that how you came to live here?"

He nodded. "They gave her the cottage to live in, but after my mother went missing, they blamed my father like everyone else. I was an adult and could take care of myself, so my father left The Cove. I haven't seen or heard from him since. I stayed in the cottage because it's the only home I've ever known and basically all I have left of either of them."

"Wow, do you still talk to your grandparents?"

"A little, but I haven't really seen much of them. I know they love me, but I look like my father. I think it's too painful for them."

"How awful. It must feel like you've lost everyone in

your life who you were close to." She looked out at the rolling waves and swallowed past the lump in her throat. "I know what it's like to lose everything."

He waited patiently, staring at her with understanding eyes, making it so easy for her to talk to him. There was just something about him that made her want to curl up in his lap and tell him all her secrets.

She took a deep breath and decided to just go for it. "Two years ago, I was doing field work with my fiancé back in Washington."

His eyes widened slightly. "You were engaged?"

She nodded. "That's why this is so hard on me."

His tone softened. "What happened?"

"We had a run in with a bear, and I did all the wrong things. Harlow saved my life. He distracted the bear and ran off in the opposite direction. I haven't seen or heard from him since, either."

Greyson's brow furrowed. "Did they track the bear?"

"They did everything." She tucked her hair behind her ear. "There was no sign of any remains. He just disappeared. It's the not knowing what happened to him that is so hard to live with."

Greyson nodded. "Same for me. Everyone copes with things differently." He studied her. "Is that why you don't drink?"

She blinked.

"When I found you in the cave, you said you felt like you had a hangover, but that wasn't possible because you didn't drink anymore."

He was observant, she'd give him that. She hadn't remembered saying that. Not that she hid it from people, but it wasn't something she went around advertising, either. She sighed. "I had a hard time when Harlow went missing, but that's not what sent me spiraling down a really bad road."

Greyson silently waited once more. No judgment, just compassion.

"I found out I was pregnant. The thought that Harlow might never get to meet his child filled me with stress, and I...I...m-miscarried." A small sob slipped out.

Greyson opened his arms, and she flew into them without hesitation. He held her for a long time while she let the tears flow. She had a family who loved and cared about her, but they worried about her, too. She didn't want to be a burden to them, so she held her feelings back and gave the appearance of being strong.

With Greyson, she felt like she could be free.

"I'm so sorry, Sparrow. That truly sucks. I'm not going to say everything is going to be okay, because I hate when people tell me that. But one thing I *do* know is that you can't blame yourself. None of this is your fault. Sometimes life is shitty, and we can't do a damn thing about it. And sometimes life is wonderful. All we can do is put one foot in front of the other and take things day by day, hoping the good ones will outweigh the bad."

"Life was good when I got here, but it turned bad pretty quickly." Her voice hitched.

He tipped her chin up. "Maybe things will get better if we stick together."

She searched his face, then pulled back. "Greyson, I don't think—"

"As friends." He stepped away and smiled but it didn't quite reach his eyes. "We seem like a good team so far, Sparrow. I think together we can figure this thing out."

"I sure hope so."

"That's all that I ask. Just keep your hope alive."

"I'll try."

"Good. It's getting late, and we have a big day tomorrow. We'd better get to bed." His gaze landed on her lips briefly, then he disappeared back into the house, and the last thing she expected to happen...happened. She felt something she never imagined she could ever feel again.

The butterflies began to dance in her stomach.

* * *

"I CAN'T BELIEVE it's been a week, and we're no closer to finding Lily than we were on day one." Sparrow looked at Laura, Stacy, Olivia, Zoe, and Tia as they stood in the packed marina of The Cove. "Something else must be done. I don't understand how everyone can just go about their lives as if nothing has happened. Lily is still out there. Alive or dead, we need to know what happened. We owe that to her parents. They need to know." *Sparrow* needed to know. She couldn't handle not knowing the fate of someone else she cared about.

"I'm so sorry." Stacy cradled her sleeping baby, snuggled in a pink Boba carrier wrapped around her body.

"The police and sheriff's departments are still looking, Sparrow. Along with the rangers and wardens. They've just called off the public search party." Laura touched her arm. "The Cove won't survive if everything stays shut down. These festivals bring in a lot of revenue to sustain the town during the long harsh winters. We can't afford not to have them, especially with all the hunters, birdwatchers, naturalists, and leaf peepers in town this time of year."

"Keeping the peace among them is not easy. Trent has his hands full." Stacy shook her head.

"Same with Hank." Olivia scanned the crowd. "Several fights have broken out in town. It's total chaos."

"You're telling me," Zoe said. "Add alcohol to the

mix, and poor Jack has had to break up his fair share of fights at The Claw."

"Alcohol doesn't mix well with opposing groups of any kind, but especially when guns are involved," Tia added.

"At least in town these disputes are easier to enforce. I can't imagine the rangers trying to keep the woods safe with over-enthusiastic nature-loving bird-watchers running into eager hunters." Laura rubbed her temples. "It's a public relations nightmare. We need these festivals to be a success. The town council is breathing down my neck, while the school board is already making requests for the spring activities. Thank the Lord my husband is helping Trent and Hank. That makes him less frustrated with my work hours at the moment with Oktoberfest kicking off the season."

Oktoberfest was a week-long festival celebrating the German culture. There were all sorts of kegs containing German beer. Food trucks with German fair lined the harbor. Larry and Buck set up the equipment for the stage where bands played, and dancers entertained in historic German fashion. There were German games, activities, and even a costume contest, and the festival ended with a parade followed by fireworks.

"I understand all of that, but I can't sit around and do nothing, even though that's what everyone is telling me to do." Sparrow looked around, scanning the crowd.

Her entire department was there, but she'd been avoiding them. No one said they blamed her for Lily's disappearance, but Sparrow had been the one in charge. Chris had questioned everything Sparrow had done in the field, and Victoria had pulled everyone from the field during the search this past week. Only now that the public search had been called off was everyone free to go back to work.

Everyone except Sparrow.

Victoria felt like she needed more time to recover, and she still didn't trust their field site area fully. Sparrow understood that, but there was no way she was going to continue doing nothing.

"You went through a lot, Sparrow. It's okay to take some time for yourself to heal." Stacy's baby stirred and started to cry.

Sparrow's gaze dropped to the baby, and her heart ached. Stacy was right. She needed to heal, and she couldn't do that here. With Greyson still out with the other law enforcement agencies searching the woods, Sparrow felt empty and alone. There was this crazy connection between them that was hard to deny.

That had never happened to her so quickly, and it terrified her.

He had become such a great support system to her so quickly, but she needed to learn to support herself. The only way she could do that was by making a difference. She was through waiting. She knew what she had to do...

And that started tonight.

10

THE NEXT DAY, Greyson was weary and tired. After Sparrow had moved in, she pulled away from him again. He'd given her space because he didn't want to scare her away, but there wasn't a day that went by that he didn't think about her. When he was with her, when he wasn't with her, it didn't matter.

She was always on his mind.

She'd been through so much. She was a fighter. He knew she could take care of herself, but the urge to wrap her in his arms and kiss her worries away hadn't dimmed a single day since she'd come into his life. If anything, it burned even stronger. He'd never realized how lonely he was before he met her.

They'd continued to search for Lily all week with the rest of the town. No one was having any luck, and the town couldn't withstand being shut down any longer. So, after Trent and Hank called off the public search, people from all the law-enforcement departments continued to divide and conquer in their search for Lily.

Greyson glanced at the late afternoon sky. He still had a few hours before the sun set. He would travel the furthest north he'd gone yet, before finding shelter for the night. He drove his ATV deeper into the woods, looking for any signs of Lily.

The ballistics report had come back on that shell casing. Trent was right. It belonged to a machine gun. Not the kind of weapon you hunted with, which made him worry even more about who was in his woods. He kept his eyes peeled when he saw something up ahead. His pulse picked up as adrenaline coursed through him.

He flipped the snap off his holster before picking up speed. The trail wound around different curves and bends to avoid trees and bushes. Finally, he broke through the trees into a clearing. He gunned his engine and tried to catch up to the person in front of him, ready to react on a moment's notice.

They passed the clearing and entered the tree line once more when the person suddenly looked over their shoulder and did a double take. Greyson reached for his gun. Almost immediately, they started to slow down. They finally pulled over off the path behind a cluster of small trees and bushes. Greyson drew his weapon as he pulled up behind the ATV. The person flipped up the visor of the helmet, and Greyson gaped.

There was no mistaking those light gray eyes.

He holstered his weapon and flipped the visor to his own helmet up. "Sparrow, what the hell are you doing way out here?" His tone sounded harsher than he'd intended, but fear tended to do that to him.

Her face flushed pink, and she sat up straighter, lifting her chin a notch. "Looking for Lily, same as you."

"These woods can be dangerous. You shouldn't—"

"If one more person says that to me, I'm going to scream. I can't sit back and do nothing, and Victoria won't let me go back to work yet. Chris is handling the field operation in Lily's and my absence."

"I'm sorry." Greyson held his hands up and slowly got off his ATV to walk over to her. "I don't mean to sound harsh, but these woods really are dangerous. Wild animals are a threat, and poachers are still around. I found several spots where they poached what they wanted and left the remains to rot. I'm sure they stole many other species to illegally sell as well. And then there's the fact that I found a shell casing to a machine gun a little while ago. Hunters don't use machine guns."

"All the more reason to find Lily."

"I agree." He tucked a strand of her hair off her cheek back into her helmet, needing to touch her in some small way. "But putting yourself in danger won't do anyone any good."

"I knew I wouldn't be in danger because I didn't plan on being alone." Her eyes met his. "I came looking for you."

His heart sped up slightly over her words, but then logic set in. She needed his help. Nothing more. He cleared his throat. "How did you know where I would be?"

"The last time you checked in with me, you said the northern woods were the only place no one had looked for Lily yet. So, I took a chance. I'm not reckless. I brought my radio in my pack. If I didn't find you soon, I had planned to radio you."

She might not be reckless, but she was emotional and too close to the situation. Emotions made a person careless.

He sighed. "Well, since you're here, we should probably get going. It's getting dark, and we need to find a place to set up camp for the night. Stay close and follow me." He waited for her to nod. Only then did he walk back to his own ATV and climb on.

He was just about to start his four-wheeler when the unmistakable sound of more ATVs came from up ahead. *Shit.* This was why he didn't want anyone with him, especially Sparrow. He quickly hopped off his four-wheeler and motioned for Sparrow to do the same and remain quiet. They still wore their packs and helmets as they crouched down behind the bushes out of sight.

A single rider came flying down the path. When the rider looked over his shoulder, he steered into a tree and went flying over the handlebars, landing about fifty feet away from them. His ATV was still running. Sparrow started to stand, but Greyson pulled her down and motioned for her to stay still and quiet. He pointed down the trail then tapped his ears for her to listen.

Above the sound of the ATV was more noise off in the distance.

Sure enough, moments later, two more ATVs arrived, stopping beside the single rider. Two huge men climbed off the four-wheelers, pulling off their helmets as they did so. The man on the ground's helmet had fallen off after he'd hit the tree. He lay there, moaning.

"Get up," one of the men who was bald said with a deep voice that rumbled. His muscles strained at the seams of his jacket.

"I-I can't," the much smaller man on the ground with a foreign accent managed to get out.

"Shoot him and leave him for the wolves," the other man who was just as big and had a tight black beard said.

"No, please." The smaller man on the ground held his hands out before him. He struggled and groaned as he rolled to his side, holding his stomach, and somehow managed to get to his feet. "I'll do whatever you want, just please don't kill me."

Sparrow gasped and both men pulled out guns as they looked around. Greyson tensed and held his breath, his heartbeat pulsing in his ears. The bearded man started walking in their direction. Greyson pulled out his own weapon, but a deer darted out of the bushes and ran past the man, making him flinch. He cursed, then rejoined the other two. Greyson nearly wilted with relief as the men turned their attention back to the man on the ground.

"Where's the rest of the money?" The bald man shoved his gun into the smaller man's chest.

"What do you mean the rest?" The smaller man took a step back.

"You tried to double-cross us." The man with a beard took a step forward. "Our boss won't be happy about that."

"I-I'm just the delivery man. My boss is the one who makes the deals. I didn't know how much money was in the bag."

"Next time, you might want to count it first." The bald man cocked his gun. "We delivered the product. You didn't deliver the money. You're short about half of what we agreed upon. Someone has to pay. Since your boss isn't here, that someone is you." He pointed the gun at the man's head.

"But if you kill me, who will send a message back to my boss."

"No need for a messenger. When your boss doesn't get the product and you don't return, he'll get the message."

"Guns are noisy," the foreign man sputtered. "Search parties are out for that missing girl. Someone will hear if you shoot me."

"Don't worry about the girl. Besides, who said anything about shooting anyone?" The man with a beard pulled out a long, deadly knife.

A flock of birds went sailing out of the bushes up through the trees, startling the big men who spun around in a circle. Sparrow jumped as well, letting out a shriek that drew the attention of the men in their direction. The smaller man took off running into the woods.

The bald man motioned for the bearded man with a knife to chase after him, while he pointed his gun and took long strides in Greyson and Sparrow's direction.

Shit.

No time to get on their ATVs. Greyson grabbed Sparrow's hand and they took off running in the opposite direction. They heard the bald man curse and start running after them. There was no way they would beat him in a foot race. Even with Greyson helping her, Sparrow's strides were too short. Their only hope of survival was to venture off the path and cut through the woods to the river.

Pulling her as fast as he could without tripping her up, Greyson led Sparrow on a zigzag path toward the edge of a cliff. A bullet whizzed past his helmet. So much for worrying about not being heard. Then again, Greyson had his ranger uniform on. Whatever the man was up to was obviously no good. It stood to reason that he wouldn't want witnesses.

He wouldn't let them live if he caught up to them.

They came to the edge of the cliff, and Sparrow dug in her heels. Greyson flipped open the visor of his helmet and she did the same.

"I can't jump. I'm scared." She panted for breath, and her eyes looked terrified.

"So am I, but we don't have a choice. We're dead otherwise. Hold my hand and don't let go, okay?"

She closed her eyes and nodded, then opened them with renewed determination as she gripped his hand tight. Looking past her, he saw the bald man stop and raise his gun.

"Now!" Greyson yelled.

They both leapt off the edge of the cliff together just as the bald man fired his gun.

* * *

"Awe, look at you. What a nice boyfriend." Zoe cleared a spot on her desk in the harbormaster's office, overlooking the marina and ocean beyond that.

"I figure if you won't take time to eat, then I'll bring the food to you." Jack set a plate of crab cakes down in front of her with a tall, iced tea.

"Have I told you lately that I love you?" She sighed dreamily, and her mouth watered as she inhaled the delicious aroma, making her realize just how hungry she was.

Crab cakes were traditionally more of a mid-Atlantic staple, but Maine's Peekytoe crabs worked just as well. Zoe loved crab meat, especially Peekytoe. The rock or sand crab's name came from the handpicked toe meat and the pointed shape of the leg.

The Peekytoe was a small crab, maybe only five inches across, with a red or orange shell and white belly. She loved that the crabmeat was shell free and ready to eat because it was picked right after it was caught. Less work for her. And the Peekytoe crab was sweet, salty, delicate, and juicy. White meat with bits of pink and a firmness to it, but it was equally delicate and silky, just the way she liked it.

"I know what my girl likes, and I love you, too." Jack laughed. "But seriously, you work too hard." He sat in the chair across from her while she ate.

"Well, that's the pot calling the kettle and all that." She grunted and kept eating. "You have like five jobs."

"I know, I just worry about you."

She paused and wiped her mouth. "I'm just trying to do my part to help Greyson out. My friends in the Coast Guard have seen an increase in activity on the water from other countries as well as our own. None of the boats have come through the marina, but you know how that is. That water is so deep along the coastline, they can pull right up next to the shore to smuggle anything they want. It's so hard to police that, but we're all doing our best."

"I know you are. I'll keep an eye out. I'm taking a group of tourists on my charter boat tomorrow afternoon to see the leaves along the shore up north."

"Oh, great. I wish I could help out, but I'm swamped here."

"That's okay. My parents are in town for the festival, so they're going to tag along and help. Mom can make her chowder, and Dad can entertain the group while I drive the boat. The weather looks good, so the trip should be a go."

"Tell your parents I said hi and let me know if you see anything."

"Will do." He picked up the dishes. "Gotta get back for the dinner crowd." He leaned over and gave her a kiss then shot her a wink and walked out the door.

Her heart warmed over at the thought that he was all hers. She couldn't help wondering when he would ask her to move in with him. They had been dating for six months. She practically lived at his apartment above the bar anyway because it was so much closer to both their jobs than her apartment was. Might as well make it official.

She knew in her heart that he was the one.

They'd both said they loved each other. If he asked her to marry him today, she would say yes, hands down. She was a modern woman. Maybe she would ask him to marry her instead. At the very least, she wanted to wake up next to him every day, but she couldn't ask him if she could move into his place. She was putting down her foot.

He had to ask her that himself.

Pulling herself away from thoughts of things she

couldn't control, she looked over the paperwork on her desk. Now this was something well within her control, she just didn't feel like tackling it. She wished they would have some luck on their side for a change.

Lily was missing still. That thought weighed heavy on everyone's minds. The woods were a mess right now, and the town was behind on all the work that needed to be done before winter. Something had to give soon.

Her radio went off, pulling her from her thoughts. She pressed the button and said, "Harbormaster Granger, here. Over," and then let go.

"Zoe, it's Merle." Merle was a member of the Coast Guard and a good friend. Zoe had known him for years. They'd gone through training together.

"Hey, Merle, what's up?"

"We got one!"

11

SPARROW SWALLOWED a mouthful of water as she struggled to stay afloat in the river. Panic threatened to consume her. Her worst nightmare had come true. The weight of her pack was heavy, but she knew she couldn't survive without the contents. Her helmet was still on her head. Rays of sunlight were dwindling as dusk was setting upon them. She blinked and squinted harder. A sob slipped out. She could see Greyson's helmet ahead of her.

He was alive.

Relief washed through her. He hadn't been shot. But her relief was short lived. The rapids carried them at a frantic pace, their helmets saving them more than once as the force of the water crashed them into rocks and tree limbs. The only good thing was the bald man with the gun was long gone.

No human could ever keep up with the fast flow of the river on foot, but she knew he and the other man would go back for their ATVs and keep looking for them in the morning. They only had tonight to be safe. Dawn would bring on the hunt, and they would be the prey. But first, they had to survive the river. A new kind of danger loomed ahead of them.

Drowning.

She plunged beneath the water again, losing more and more strength along the way. One of her biggest fears was drowning. She'd nearly drowned as a child and had been traumatized ever since. The thought of holding her breath until her head felt like it would explode, and then gasping for air only to have her lungs fill with icy cold water until her heart stopped and her organs shut down, gave her nightmares.

Dying in a cold, dark, watery grave was horrifying.

She blinked, realizing she wasn't dead yet and didn't want to be. If she didn't drown, hypothermia would get her for sure. The water was dark, with bubbles and debris churning past her at a furious rate, making her disoriented.

She had too much to live for.

Kicking hard, she resurfaced and gasped for air. Blinking water out of her eyes, she looked ahead and could have cried. Greyson had made it to the side of the river. He clung to a long branch for dear life. Searching the water, his gaze locked with hers, and he stuck his arm out.

With the last shred of strength she had, she paddled hard toward the side as the river propelled her forward. She needed to get close enough, or she would miss him. And if she missed him, there was no way he would catch up to her.

It was now or never.

With the last bit of the strength she possessed, she gave one final surge forward and grabbed his outstretched hand. Her heartbeat thundered in her ears, and she gasped for every breath. His eyes held intense relief. The roar of the river was so loud, neither attempted to speak. He started to pull her toward him, when the unthinkable happened.

Her fingers started to slip from his grasp.

They froze and their eyes locked. His widened, and she could see the genuine fear in them. Fear and something more. That's when it hit her. She had been holding herself back from falling for him over a sense of guilt for a past that no longer existed. And now she was about to lose what she'd never given a chance to blossom.

She vowed if she made it out of this alive, she would show him how she felt.

He clutched at her hand to no avail. Her fingers kept slipping. Horror hit her that she actually might not make it. She stared at him, wanting his face to be the last thing she saw. Their fingertips touched one last time. She screamed his name as her hand slipped free.

His lips formed the word, *No!*

The water yanked her away, and her head sank beneath the surface. His face stayed with her in her mind's eye, and her body wilted, when suddenly she was yanked back hard. Her head popped back up out of the water, and she went into a coughing fit. A tree branch had snagged her pack. Tears streamed from her eyes as she sobbed.

She wasn't going to die.

Moments later, Greyson came running into view from down the shoreline. This time he reached for her pack instead of her hand and tugged her free of the branch, then pulled her out of the water. They both lay panting on the shore for several minutes.

Greyson rolled to his feet, then reached down and helped her to stand.

"I can't. I'm so tired." She could barely speak.

"I know. Me, too. Have to get warm. Sun's almost down." He tugged her with him into the woods.

He was right. She shook the cobwebs from her brain and walked with him as they looked around, searching until they found a good spot to camp. She pointed to a half circle of large boulders, and he nod-ded. Their small, personal tents had ripped off their packs, so they had to make do with what they had.

They both dug into their packs and pulled out their sleeping bags. He unzipped their waterproof plastic bags and pulled both their thermal sleeping bags out. He unrolled them next to the boulders, so they would have protection behind and to the sides of them.

She knew what he was thinking, and it was smart, but the thought of sharing body heat between the sleeping bags made her shiver even more. Neither of them spoke as they worked together quickly. In front of them, he knelt down with his pack once more and pulled out supplies while she gathered some nearby kindling and wood to build a fire.

The bad guys were far enough away so they wouldn't see it, and it would help keep wild animals away. Not to mention, they needed the heat to dry their clothes and warm their bodies if they were going to stay alive.

Once the fire was roaring, they stood awkwardly facing each other. He started to strip off his clothes. She tried, but her hands shook so hard. He paused and his eyes dropped to her chattering teeth, which spurred him into motion.

Within seconds, he stood in front of her. Quickly and efficiently, he removed all her clothing except her bra and underwear and hung them on branches by the fire. Helping her between the sleeping bags, he quickly removed the rest of his own clothing except his boxer briefs and hung them all by the fire as well, then he joined her.

Wrapping his arms and legs around her body, she couldn't help but sigh over the heat radiating between them. It took a while, but finally her body stopped shiv-ering. She melted into him. She knew tomorrow their brief reprieve would be over, but for now, she basked in the feeling of being warm, safe, protected…

Alive.

* * *

GREYSON AWOKE at dawn's first light, feeling the heat of soft flesh wrapped tightly around him. His arms were wrapped around a slender body with one hand resting on the curve of a buttocks and the other threaded through silky strands of hair that belonged to the head resting on his bare chest. His pectoral muscle twitched and full lips brushed against it, causing his penis to stir to life as the catlike body stretched against him.

His eyes flew open.

Sparrow's pale gray eyes stared up at him.

He didn't dare move for fear he was dreaming. She was awake, and in his arms, and looking at him with desire blazing from her eyes. She watched him as she slowly kissed his chest again, making her message clear.

"Sparrow," he whispered.

"Shhh," she said softly and rolled on top of him.

He sucked in a breath as her small, perfect breasts pressed against his chest and her slender legs slid over his sides until she straddled him. He let out a hiss but didn't move, giving her the option to stop any time she wanted, even if it would kill him. He squeezed his eyes shut, fisting his hands as he fought for control.

Full lips kissed his face softly until his own lips parted, then she pressed her mouth against his. Passion shot through his every cell. He understood her need. They had cheated death a couple times, and with the dawn came the realization that they were alive. A need to *feel* alive possessed him, too.

No questions asked.

He would work out what exactly that meant later. All thoughts but her faded away. Running his hands over her back, he slipped his thumbs between their bodies and beneath her bra to skim her nipples. She cried out against his lips and kissed him deeper. He slid his palms down her sides and along her legs then up the backs of her thighs and beneath her panties.

His fingertips caressed her bare bottom until she squirmed, grinding hard against his arousal. He moaned against her lips, plunging his tongue deep as his fingers traveled lower and he slipped one then two inside of her. She whimpered in pleasure.

God, she was so wet and hot and expressive.

It had been a while for him, and he nearly lost it. Stroking her deeper and deeper as his tongue stroked every inch of her mouth, he wanted more. She seemed to sense his need and had the same urgency that he did. Reaching between them, she stroked the length of him as she slid his boxers down and then slipped her panties to the side, guiding him into her.

He couldn't help himself. He tugged on her panties until they ripped and then plunged deeper inside of her until he was fully immersed. They both stilled until their bodies adjusted. Her heat pulsed over his throbbing penis. He cursed, clenching his jaw for control.

She lifted her head and looked him in the eyes then clenched, squeezing him internally until he thought he would explode. His hands gripped her ass, and he dove his tongue deep between her lips.

That was her undoing.

She started moving her hips frantically. He stilled her movements and rolled them to the side, lifting one of her legs higher as he slowly slid the long length of his thick penis in and out of her fully, over and over until she clawed at him for more.

She was amazing.

A goddess who wore her every emotion on her face, in her movements, in her little sighs and shivers. He couldn't hold back anymore. He quickened the pace, faster and faster, until she flipped him back over and rode him hard. His hands slid to her hips to help her move even faster until they were both panting and sweating in unison.

Pressure built, and he didn't know how much longer he could last. She whipped her head back and forth and let her orgasm overtake her, arching her back on top of him and calling out his name as she collapsed against his chest. Only then did he pull out at the last second, his body seizing with his own release.

She went limp in his arms, her head resting on his chest, and they both lay there silent and content for several moments. He stroked her back softly, and she ran her fingertips over his chest, lightly scratching him with her nails.

The noises of birds and animals awakening sounded in the forest, and reality returned.

"We should probably get dressed." Sparrow sat up.

"Right." Greyson did the same.

What the hell had just happened?

His mind was buzzing. He rationalized there had been an unspoken need between the two of them after all they had been through. He didn't know if she still thought of him as only a friend, and he still didn't want to pressure her. If he were honest, they were in uncharted territory. He had no idea what to say or do.

Not to mention, they were still in danger.

Once again, he decided to let her take the lead. There would be time enough later to sort out the details of what had just happened between them. All he knew for certain was that he would never be the same. His little songbird had changed him.

Sparrow was special.

She had awakened a burning need for her within his soul. There was no going back for him. No one else would do. He wanted her. *All* of her. Heart, mind, body, soul. He was a patient man. He knew she felt the connection between them, too.

She had to.

He had felt it from the moment he'd met her, but she had fought it. He now knew that was out of fear of getting hurt again and guilt and loyalty to her long-lost fiancé because she didn't have closure. She shouldn't have to wait around forever to start living again. Greyson vowed right then and there, no matter how long it took...

He would prove to her they were meant to be together.

They quickly got dressed and repacked their backpacks, which had also dried out. They ate the nutrition bars from their packs and drank water from their canteens. She kept stealing glances at him, but she remained quiet. He could tell she wanted to say something, but she didn't. Since she was the one to initiate making love, he wasn't about to guess at why?

He wasn't a mind reader.

He pulled out his radio and just as he'd figured, it was ruined. "How's your radio?" he asked.

Sparrow jumped at the sound of his voice, then her cheeks flushed pink. She dug in her bag and pulled hers out. Testing it, she shook her head. "Mine's ruined as well. I'm not surprised. Thrashing about in river rapids and smashing into rocks would ruin the toughest of equipment."

He cursed softly. "There's no way to call for help." He scanned the area, looking for signs of anything familiar. "I'm not exactly sure where we are. The river took us a little further south, but I'm guessing we're still in the northern woods. If we stick to the river and keep heading south, that should take us to some field sites. At least our odds will be better of running into the kind of people we want to."

"Those men will most likely follow the river, knowing it would take us south. And they have ATVs."

"True, but they will go slow and search along the riverbank. Besides, we'll hear them coming before we see them and can hide if we have to. For now, let's follow the river. We still have our supplies, so I'm not worried about surviving."

"What about animals?" She looked around nervously as they walked. "Animals come to the water to drink and catch fish." She glanced at him. "I'm not overly fond of bears after what happened."

His voice softened with understanding and compassion. "That's understandable. I think we'll be fine. I still have my gun. It should fire even after getting wet. I drained the water last night, so it should be dry."

They kept walking along the river, making small talk about all sorts of things but avoiding any mention of what had happened only a couple of hours ago. It was eating him alive, but he'd be damned if he would be the one to say something first. Every time he'd tried in the past, she'd shot him down. This time, she would have to make the first move.

They walked a little more, then Sparrow stopped.

He glanced back at her. "Is something wrong?"

"No...yes...I don't know. I'm not very good at this." She bit her bottom lip.

His heart melted. "You're doing just fine," he said, waiting patiently, but his heart had picked up its pace, wondering what she was about to say.

"Well, I—"

A thrashing sounded in the trees just beyond them so suddenly, neither of them had a chance to react.

"Oh, God, it's a bear." Sparrow stood tall, putting her arms up high and making herself look big.

Maine didn't have Grizzly bears and those were the only bears you crouched down on the ground into a ball in front of, covering your neck with your hands and staying small. For all other bears, you stood tall and made noise.

Unless it was a mama with bear cubs, then you were screwed.

"Put your arms down, Sparrow." Greyson reached out to take her hand. "It's not a bear. It's worse."

"What's worse than a bear?"

"Two bull moose fighting during the rut." He looked at her. "Run!"

Too late.

Two moose emerged with antlers locked, stomping and snorting and pawing at each other. They finally broke free, and one ran off. The other stood far too close to Greyson and Sparrow. They had the river behind them and no desire to go back into that, but they would have to get past the moose to hide behind a tree. They were out in the open and vulnerable to this majestic creature's will.

This moose stood around six feet tall at the shoulder, a majestic tower of muscle with a rack that had to be about five feet in width. Moose weren't always aggressive towards humans, but cows could be aggressive when protecting their calves. And bull moose could be downright terrifying during the rut.

Mating season was no joke.

Greyson noticed the long hairs on its hump were raised and his ears were laid back, a clear sign of agitation. The bull licked its lips, warning them they were way too close. It took a couple steps slowly towards them, but there was no place to back away to.

"What do we do?" Sparrow whispered. "There's nothing to hide behind."

"Many times their charges are only bluffs, warning people to stay away. I sure as hell don't want to call that bluff. We need to put something between us and this big guy or run away. Moose don't chase you very far."

The bull took another step towards them.

"Oh, God, it's going to charge, isn't it?" Sparrow wrung her hands together and whispered, "It's just like before."

The moose started snorting and acting more agitated. She was right. Greyson made a decision. He had to get the moose away from her, at any cost. He couldn't bear it if he lost her. He dropped his pack on the ground and sprinted around the moose, shouting for Sparrow to run for the trees and take cover.

The moose took the bait and ran after him.

He ran for the trees, but the moose knocked him down before he could reach one. It started stomping and kicking with all four of its feet. Pain sliced through Greyson, making it hard to breathe. He managed to curl up into a ball and protect his head with his hands the best he could, holding as still as possible until it stopped. He didn't move or try to get up and prayed Sparrow knew enough to stay silent and hidden.

The last thing he needed was for the moose to renew its attack.

He wouldn't survive if that happened. Every muscle, tendon, bone, and organ in his body ached, and his head pounded in agony. He felt blood dripping down his temple, and his vision grew blurry. He felt like he was going to be sick.

Finally, the moose ran off.

Greyson groaned. That was all he could manage. He heard footsteps running. Sparrow crouched down to his side and touched his back. He let out a whimper.

"Oh, God, you're bleeding in so many spots. Greyson, talk to me, please. Can you hear me? Are you okay?" Her voice was strong, but he could hear her underlying fear.

He tried to speak, but no words came out. He fell over to his side and saw her tear-stained face seconds before the world around him went black.

12

"GREYSON! WAKE UP, PLEASE." Sparrow patted his cheeks.

She was still in shock. Everything had happened so quickly. One minute she was getting ready to tell him how she felt about him and what making love had meant to her, then the next thing she knew, a bull moose was charging them. She couldn't believe he'd drawn the bull moose away from her, same as Harlow had drawn the Grizzly bear away from her. Except, Harlow had disappeared after that, but Greyson was still here.

She would be damned if she would let history repeat itself.

Rummaging through her pack, she pulled out her first aid kit. Greyson lay unconscious on his back. She undid his ranger coat and shirt, then probed his ribs. She was no expert, but she was guessing his ribs were cracked. Bruises were already forming. As carefully as she could, she wrapped the bandage around him, which wasn't easy since he couldn't help, and then she fastened it.

He would be in agony when he woke up, and she didn't have anything strong to give him. Over-the-counter pain pills would have to do. The back of his head had a gash on it. She put disinfectant and gauze over it and wrapped it up, but worried he might have a concussion. She treated a few other cuts and surveyed her work.

That was the best she could for now.

She carefully rebuttoned his shirt and zipped his jacket. The wind picked up, and storm clouds were rolling in once more. What else could they possibly go through? He was too heavy for her to move, and they were vulnerable out in the open by the river.

They had to keep moving.

She needed to make a travois pull-sled to pull Greyson to a safer location. She rummaged through her pack, but she only had a Ka-Bar machete. That would work but would use up most of her energy. She took a chance and looked in Greyson's pack. A sigh of relief slipped out. He had a pocket chain saw encased in a protective, waterproof case. She glanced over at him, still lying there unconscious. She hated to leave him, but she had no choice.

Sparrow quickly ventured into the woods and looked for two twelve-to-fifteen-foot hardwood trees to use as poles. Given Greyson's tall height, she figured the longer she could find, the better. It didn't take long to find two dead trees around the right length. She used the mini chain saw to cut off the ends. Then she did the same with three shorter trees around five foot each to use as cross bars.

Gathering her branches, she returned to Greyson's side and laid them out on the ground. She trimmed the cross poles, so they would be bigger at the bottom and tapered to smaller at the top. After placing the two long trees down, she crossed them at the top, creating a two-foot overlap on the narrower end of both trees, creating an X shape. The bottom ends were spaced wider apart, creating a Tipi look. Using cordage from both of their packs, she secured the branches in a tapering fashion the rest of the way up the ladder about six inches apart and narrowing.

A gust of wind stirred up pine needles, grass, and dirt around her. She flipped her travois frame over and used the mini chain saw to carve a smooth surface like a ski so the pull-sled would slide with ease over the ground. She flipped her sled back over, and with more of the cord, she rigged up a sling so more of the weight would be distributed across her shoulders and not all on her hands, adding an extra piece of Greyson's clothing to use as padding.

Spreading one of their sleeping bags out over the travois, she carefully rolled Greyson on top of it. Using what was left of their cords, she tied him to it and secured their packs to it as well. With the physics of the travois, and the help of the sling, she was able to lift the pull-sled and pull it behind her as she walked.

She kept walking and taking breaks for what felt like forever, stopping to eat and drink. Greyson still hadn't woken up, which concerned her. He moaned here and there, but when she held her hand to his forehead, he didn't feel like he had a fever. The clouds were getting more ominous, but she had to stay by the river, so she would know for sure what direction she was going. Although the sled moved easier on flat ground than through the woods, but she was terrified the bad guys would catch up to her.

Or another wild animal.

She had pulled Greyson's gun out during one of her breaks and put it in her coat along with bear spray. If anything happened, she would be prepared. She had no sooner had thought that when she heard sounds coming from the woods.

Quickly setting Greyson down, she placed herself

between him and the woods. She reached in her pocket just as a man stepped out of the woods. She pulled the gun out of her pocket. She knew how to use a gun; she just didn't own one herself.

She sucked in a breath. "You!"

The wild man stood before her, still dressed in camo, and wearing a pack of his own. His long hair was pulled into a low ponytail and his beard was trimmed shorter. He didn't look at her. His eyes were trained on Greyson.

"Why did you drug me?" she asked.

"It wasn't a drug. It was medicinal tea to help you relax and heal."

"Relax? It knocked me out cold."

"What's wrong with him?" he asked, his stare intense.

"Where's Lily?" Sparrow ignored his question.

He took a step forward.

She cocked the gun.

That got his attention. His gaze snapped up to hers, and he froze. "I'm not going to hurt you or him."

"I don't believe you. She never drank the tea, and neither did you. When I woke up, Lily was missing, and you were gone. So, I repeat, where is she?"

The sky grew darker. He glanced at it with a frown before responding. "When I left, Lily was sleeping in the cave, same as you. I didn't take her, and I don't know where she is. You need to get him to a shelter before the rain comes."

"Don't worry about him. Let me have your radio. I know you have one."

"That's a good idea. You shouldn't be out here." He reached for his pack.

"Slowly," she said, thrusting the gun out further.

He slowed his movements and set the pack on the

ground. Unzipping it, he pulled out a two-way radio just like Greyson's and hers.

"Set it on the ground and back away."

He did as she asked.

She quickly grabbed the radio and was about to turn it on and call for help when Greyson stirred.

The wild man took a step toward Greyson, and Sparrow pointed the gun at him again. "Don't go near him."

The man held his hands up before him. "I just want to make sure he's all right."

"Why do you care?"

Greyson opened his eyes at that moment and spoke for the first time since he'd been trampled by the moose. He turned his head and looked at the wild man with wide, confused eyes as he said with a hoarse voice, "Dad?"

* * *

GREYSON SAT PROPPED against a cave wall, staring in disbelief at the man before him. Right after he'd asked him if he was his father, the clouds burst open, and rain began to fall. The man had grabbed the travois and started quickly pulling him into the woods with Sparrow hot on his heels. She still held Greyson's gun and kept it trained on the man, but even she seemed to realize he could pull the sled faster than she could.

Now that they were safe and dry in a cave, Greyson had untied himself and sat up. Sparrow looked in shock as she sat beside him with the gun in one hand and the radio in the other. She looked at Greyson with wide, questioning eyes.

"This is your father?" she asked in barely more than a whisper.

"He looks different, but I would know my own father anywhere." Greyson stared him down as anger filled him. "Why, Dad?"

His father gazed at him with a mixture of regret and fondness. "I'm sorry, son. I know that probably doesn't mean much to you. When your mother disappeared, everyone thought I had something to do with it. I loved your mother. I would never do anything to hurt her. When they couldn't prove anything, they let the case go cold."

"I know all of that. Why did you leave?"

"They might have let the case go cold, but I couldn't. You were an adult, so I figured you didn't need me. And I wasn't good to anyone without my Carolyn. I refused to believe she was dead, and I've been looking for her ever since."

"You're wrong, Dad. I did still need you. I haven't heard from you in five years. I felt like I lost both Mom and you. Do you know what that has been like for me?"

"I'm so sorry, Grey."

"Sorry isn't enough."

"I don't want to interrupt, but we should call for help." Sparrow touched Greyson's arm. "Those bad guys are still out there, and you need medical attention."

"She's right, son. You need to stay far away from this section of the woods."

"These are *my* woods. What the hell is going on, Dad? Are you involved with these men?"

"No, I promise." His father shook his head, his face transforming with determination. "I've been looking for your mother."

"Do you think they took her?"

His featured hardened. "Maybe. Same as Lily."

"Then you need to come with us and talk to the sheriff and chief," Sparrow said. "It's dangerous out here for you, too."

His father glanced at her. "I can't."

"Why not?" Greyson asked, growing frustrated with him.

"I can't tell you that." He paused a beat. "You have to trust me."

A harsh laugh slipped out of Greyson's mouth. "I don't have to do anything you tell me to do." He felt a muscle in his jaw pulse before he added, "You lost that privilege five years ago."

"When this is all over with, I'll tell you everything. I promise I won't lose touch again. Until then, don't worry about me." His father pulled out his compass and read off their coordinates to Sparrow, then slipped the device back into his pack and started to back away toward the cave entrance.

"You aren't going anywhere." Greyson took the gun from Sparrow. "I'm not playing around, Dad. We need your help, and so does Lily."

"I can't. I'm sorry, son. You'll know why soon. Stay safe." With one last look, he slipped out of the cave.

His father knew, as well as Greyson did, that he would never shoot him. But Greyson couldn't help wondering if he would ever see him again.

* * *

DAMMIT, this whole situation was getting out of control.

I stood in the woods, just out of sight, the acid burning a hole through my stomach. How had things gone so wrong so quickly? The rain was coming down heavier now. I'd made a phone call to handle this so I didn't have to, but search and rescue had shown up before Greyson and Sparrow could be disposed of.

They were getting too close to the truth, and I couldn't have that.

Those fucking idiots had shot at them even after they had specifically been told not to fire any weapons. They were supposed to be skilled enough individuals to handle any witnesses without the use of a gun. That was a joke.

I never should have let Lily live.

If the people I was involved with knew I had her and she had seen them, it would ruin everything. They would no longer trust me, and I'd worked too hard to build that trust over the years. Not to mention, they would consider me a loose end that needed to be disposed of, too. I had too much to lose to let that happen.

Then there was the river.

The rapids and sharp rocks should have been a death trap and taken care of Sparrow and Greyson. Then my hands would still be clean. The two knew what they were doing when it came to survival. Now the sheriff and police would know about the men in the woods and their suspicious activity.

I never should have gotten involved with amateurs.

I had hoped the moose attack would at least do one of them in, but no. They were the fucking luckiest pair of human beings I had ever seen. Sparrow was a god-damn MacGyver. They told the police that wild man had helped to rescue them, but they claimed not to know who he was. That just added one more person for me to dispose of.

What the hell was he doing alone in the woods, anyway?

Fucking Tarzan needed to get eaten by wolves.

I knew people who could make that happen. Too many people were searching for Lily now. I needed to make some more phone calls. Operations needed to stop for a while, but I wasn't the only one involved, even though I had the most to lose. I needed to get back to town and do some damage control.

I ducked farther back into the woods. They were moving Greyson and Sparrow out of the cave and would be heading back to town shortly. I needed to get there first. Doubling back the way I came, I would be quicker as one to their many.

Greyson would be laid up for a while, so he wasn't much of a worry anymore. Maybe if I upped my warnings for Sparrow to back off, she would finally get the message. She was an unpredictable wild card. She never listened to anyone, and that was a problem.

Maybe it was time I took matters into my own hands.

* * *

LILY HAD FALLEN into a routine she feared would never end.

Early morning every day her kidnapper came. She knew it was the same person because she kept smelling that same weird smell she couldn't place. They fed her a breakfast sandwich. Bacon, egg, and cheese on a plain bagel that she could have sworn came from The Lost Horizon. The diner always smelled of delicious bacon, and the sandwich was her favorite.

How could the person know that?

They kept her blindfolded with her hands and feet tied, only removing the rag in her mouth to feed her and give her water. She asked questions, but they refused to speak. She couldn't tell if the person was a man or a woman, and she couldn't place what that smell was that seemed familiar but just out of her reach.

They guided her to a single stall bathroom in the back of the building and pulled down her pants so she could go. She was mortified that they stood there while she went, but she had to go too badly to refuse.

The same routine happened at night, but with a lobster roll from The Claw. There was no mistaking that mouthwatering seafood smell. Again, one of her favorites. Anyone who knew her knew that she loved lobster rolls. Then again, everyone in town knew her well. And those who didn't only had to ask. With her missing, she was sure people were talking about her, so it wouldn't be that hard to learn a few of her habits. But it just seemed odd someone would kidnap her and then buy her favorite foods for her.

It was like they felt guilty or something.

She was so confused. Why feel guilty and not let her go? Why keep her around all this time? Why not just kill her? Or ask for a ransom and let her go? Why save her from those men in the woods if they were only going to kidnap her themselves? And how did this person know the men in the woods?

It was clear by their agitated movements lately, that whoever this person was, they were getting frustrated and growing tired of this game. Which left her biggest question yet...

What would happen to her next?

13

Trent stood with Hank outside of the harbormaster office in the marina, talking with Zoe that evening. The sun had set early, and the temperatures had dropped considerably, but the rain had finally stopped. The three of them headed over to The Claw for a beer. Frankly, Trent could use one.

He was thankful to have reached Greyson and Sparrow in time.

The day before, all the law enforcement departments had been searching for Lily. Then, suddenly, Greyson went dark. No one could reach him or track his location. It was like he had just disappeared. So, they returned to The Cove only to find out Sparrow, her pack, a company vehicle, and an ATV were missing as well.

Everyone knew Sparrow hadn't liked being left out of the search. She'd made that abundantly clear to everyone. Putting two and two together, her boss had figured she'd gone rogue and went looking for Lily on her own. It had been too dark to do anything about it then, but they had planned on heading out first thing in the morning.

That radio call had been music to his ears.

Walking through the doors of The Claw, soft rock music poured out of the sound system while a reality fishing show played silently on the TV. Eugene sat front and center in his usual spot at the bar. Trent let Zoe lead the way, followed by Hank, and he brought up the rear. They each took a seat at the full bar, since Jack had saved three seats for them after Zoe texted him that they were on their way.

Trent scanned the room like he always did after years of needing to be aware of his surroundings. Greggor waved to him as he left with his hunting party, glaring at Nigel and his nature loving group as he passed them on his way out the door. At least they weren't disturbing the peace anymore. Trent and Hank had enough on their plates to worry about without babysitting those two groups. He'd be glad when fall ended and the activities died down so the town could go back to normal.

Jack expertly slid a beer in front of each one of them without spilling a single drop, even in the soft lighting. "Rough day?"

"You could say that." Hank took a long swig of his beer.

"*Good* day." Trent nodded. "First one since we found both Greyson and Sparrow alive."

"Rough days for sure for Lily." Zoe shook her head. "What is happening in our woods?"

"Nothing good by the sounds of it." Jack grunted.

"The live animals and other animal parts have been recovered from the boat my Coast Guard friend intercepted and returned to the rangers." Zoe sipped her beer. "Any luck with the poachers on board? They have to be working with someone."

Trent shook his head. "They're not in charge, and they know enough not to talk. They won't give up who trafficked the animals and parts to them. The consequences would be worse than we could ever dole out."

"Greyson and Sparrow said that the wild man she and Lily had met in the woods previously showed up and helped them survive, but they also said they didn't know who he was," Hank added. "I was an FBI profiler. I can tell when someone's not being fully honest with me, though I can't imagine why either of them would feel the need to hold information back." He rubbed his jaw and squinted. "Maybe I'm reading too much into it."

Trent shrugged. "Maybe." He rolled his head on his shoulders to relieve his aching neck. These tense situations were getting to him. He'd gotten out of the military and FBI to enjoy a quieter life, but lately, life had been anything but quiet. "I'm more concerned with who those two men on ATVs and the foreign guy were."

"Maybe they have something to do with the illegal animal trafficking," Zoe speculated. "Especially since the guys on the boat were foreign as well."

"International trafficking of any kind is big money, especially across this loosely patrolled vast border." Hank took another draw from his longneck bottle. "I wish there was a way to better police it."

"You and me both." Zoe sighed. "You know how it is. The shoreline's the same way. Vast, with deep water, so boats can pull right up to it. With Nova Scotia across the way, all sorts of smuggling happens. It's impossible for any of us to catch everything."

"All we can do is our best, and that starts with finding Lily." Hank blew out his breath. "The more time that goes by, the more worried I am that we'll be too late. What if the men on the boat are connected to the men in the woods? I'm thinking any of them might have her, and no good can come from that. I wouldn't be surprised if the men in the woods killed the foreign man Greyson and Sparrow saw run from them. Hell, the men almost killed Greyson and Sparrow as well. Those two were lucky the river was that close to them, or they never would have outrun the men on foot."

"They're lucky they survived that river. The rapids are fierce." Trent finished the rest of his beer. "All I know is Greyson especially is damned lucky to be alive. A bull moose stomping on your torso isn't something most people could survive."

"No kidding." Hank took a drink of his beer. "Doc said he has several cracked ribs and a concussion. He was lucky Sparrow was with him and knew what to do. That pull-sled was impressive."

Zoe raised her beer in salute. "*She's* impressive."

"Cheers to that." Jack clinked his water glass to Zoe's beer bottle. "All our women are impressive." He winked at Zoe then took a sip.

"Damn straight, and don't you forget it." She laughed and sipped her own beer.

Hank chuckled. "I know better than to argue with that."

They all sat in silence, pondering all the madness in their town, and finishing their beers.

"Greyson said he talked to the people Lily knew in town, but no one stands out as someone who would want to do her harm." Trent set money down on the bar. "Maybe it's time we talked to some of the strangers in town this time of year. They might be a part of what's going on in the woods."

"True." Zoe looked at Trent. "Maybe Lily stepped outside that morning and saw something she shouldn't have so they took her."

"That's a possibility," he replied. "All I know is we need answers soon. I'll have my deputies start asking around."

"Roger that. I'll have my patrol officers ask around

as well." Hank dropped his own money on the bar and tapped it. "Thanks, Jack. Gotta get home to dinner. Olivia makes a mean beef stew." He tipped his hat as he stood.

"I hear that. Stacy will be looking for me to relieve her of Princess Lizzie while she cooks dinner. We'll catch up tomorrow." Trent waved and headed out of the bar to his car. It had been a rough day, indeed, and it wasn't over yet. He still had a phone call to make. Someone had some explaining to do.

Because Trent could only hide the truth for so long.

* * *

Sparrow left the hospital, exhausted. She'd had to answer to Victoria for taking a truck and a four-wheeler without permission. Victoria didn't fire her, which she'd have had every right to, but she did suspend Sparrow for two weeks. Chris would handle the field site in her absence.

Victoria hadn't let her go back to work after the first thunderstorm yet anyway, so this suspension wasn't much different. She was thankful Victoria had been so understanding. Sparrow knew she had pushed her boss' limits about as far as they would go this time.

Treading lightly, she'd avoided her as much as possible.

The girls had all shown up to check in on both her and Greyson. They had been worried sick and refused to accept Sparrow was okay without seeing for themselves and offering to stay with her. Sparrow only had a few scrapes and bruises, so she was free to go, but she told them she just needed time to be alone and process everything that had happened.

The doctors were keeping Greyson overnight to monitor his concussion because he'd been unconscious for so long. They wanted to make sure he didn't have a brain bleed. If all went well, she could bring him home the next day.

They didn't have any food in the house because she had planned on joining him in the search for Lily and staying in the woods. She'd never imagined she'd nearly die in the process and now need to take care of Greyson. She was still worried sick about Lily, and with Greyson's condition so serious, she was worried about him, too.

How much was one person supposed to *mentally* take?

Pulling into the parking lot of Gilbert's Grocery, Sparrow cut the engine to her car. She had no idea what to get. She admittedly ate like a bird because she wasn't domesticated at all, and terrible with manmade items. She'd already had to call Larry the time she plugged Greyson's sink when he was gone. He'd been busy, so more and more Buck had been the one helping her out. He always smelled of gas or some kind of fuel from fixing machines. He was a big man around her age with jet black hair.

A good-looking man, but kind of quiet and hard to get to know.

Heading inside the store, she tried to remember the things her mother used to make. Her mother, Phoenix, was a yoga instructor and a great cook. So was Sparrow's sister, River, who was an environmental activist. Even her brother, Wolf, who was a politician, could cook despite his name.

But Sparrow had only been interested in the outdoors like her father, Cliff, who wasn't domesticated in the least. He was a marine biologist and gone for long periods of time on the Pacific Ocean, which was lonely for her mother, but Sparrow understood the call of the wild.

Except Sparrow had preferred land animals after nearly drowning on a boat with him when she was little and fell overboard. They were all free spirits, but she was the only one who was as domestically challenged as her father, much to her mother's dismay.

Grabbing a cart, she headed around the outskirts of the store. She knew at least that much from her mother. That unprocessed, healthy food was on the perimeter of the store and not in the aisles. Though Sparrow couldn't seem to gain weight if she tried. So, she didn't try.

She just ate whatever was easy and convenient and took her vitamins.

But Greyson needed to heal. Which meant she needed to feed him well and take care of him. So, around the store she went, tossing in items that looked healthy. She'd have to consult with the girls on recipes or bribe them to make meals for her.

She was about to pass another aisle when she heard voices she recognized. Stopping her cart, she peeked around the corner and saw the other biologists, Ozzy and Peter. They stood talking to Willy, Greyson's assistant. She'd seen him around but hadn't officially met him yet. She couldn't hear what they said, but after a few moments, they left.

Sparrow wheeled her cart down the aisle until she caught up with him. He looked like he was about to leave. "Willy, wait. Can I have a minute of your time?"

He stopped in his tracks and faced her, his eyebrows shooting up high. "Sure. Sparrow, right?"

"Yes, it's nice to finally meet you."

"Same here. I'm so glad you and Greyson are okay. I got freaked out when we couldn't get ahold of him yesterday. Everyone was worried until you made the call today. He was lucky you were with him. I heard about the pull-sled you made. That's so cool."

"Thanks. I'm glad I could help, but trust me, I'm the lucky one. He saved my life." She swallowed hard. "I nearly drowned in the river. We wouldn't have made it out without each other, that's for sure."

Willy's expression turned serious, and his brow pinched. "Yeah, the woods can be dangerous this time of year."

"So, I've heard, and now experienced." She let out a slightly hysterical laugh. She would need daily therapy sessions after all this.

"Well, I'd better run." He started to push his cart.

"Hey, before you go, I'm curious about something."

"About what?" He looked at her with raised eyebrows.

"I saw you talking to those biologists. If you don't mind my asking, how do you know them?"

Willy looked confused for a moment, then he blinked. "Oh, yeah, those guys. Greyson has us interviewing people Lily ran into, so I was just talking to them about her. Seeing if they know anything."

"And?"

He shrugged. "They claim they don't know anything. I have to say I believe them. They don't seem like liars." He shrugged. "Well, I really do have to go. My mom's making dinner. It was nice meeting you, though. I hope Greyson gets better soon. He's a good dude." Willy walked off at a quick pace.

"Hey wait. You left your…"

Too late. He'd already exited the store, forgetting his shopping cart in the aisle. Greyson wasn't kidding. The man really wasn't that smart. She finished filling her cart and then checked out. Storing her groceries in her car, she headed home.

It was weird to call Greyson's house her home, but that's what it felt like.

She traveled the roads, mindlessly driving home,

more tired than she had felt in years. The past couple days had taken their toll on her. And she wondered what it would be like to live with Greyson now that they had made love and still hadn't talked about it. Would it be awkward? Would they make love again? She would never know for sure what had happened to her fiancé, but that had been two years ago.

It was time to move on. Hadn't she been punished enough?

She had mourned and grieved enough over the loss of him and their child. She was finally getting her life back on track. She deserved to be happy again, and Greyson made her happy. She had been trying to find the words to tell him that when the bull moose had appeared and attacked him.

Never in her wildest dreams had she imagined that as a possibility.

She was so grateful he was alive. Maybe it was time to let someone in. Let someone help her, and trust that she didn't have to be alone. As soon as she got him home, she planned to tell him exactly how she was feeling.

She came upon the last bend in the road before the turnoff to his *cottage*. Suddenly, a man stood in the middle of the road. He was average height and a little softer in the middle than she remembered, with blond hair a bit longer than Harlow Rigsby used to wear, but she would recognize him anywhere. She suddenly realized she was about to hit him.

Harlow!

She swerved to miss him and spun three-hundred-sixty degrees until she came to a stop in a ditch, dirt flying everywhere. Breathing heavy, she strove hard not to hyperventilate as she sat there and waited for the world around her to settle. She needed a minute to process what had just happened.

She was okay.

She closed her eyes and relived everything as if in slow motion. Her eyes sprang open as she remembered her vision and quickly climbed out of the car which was tilted on its side. Running up the embankment, she scanned the road.

Nothing.

She started to cry.

Maybe she was losing her mind. She had been imagining seeing him for a while now. She really needed to call her therapist. Maybe getting close to Greyson was making her feel guilty because she never had closure with Harlow. Was he alive still?

She had no clue, and that was the problem.

Taking a deep breath, she knew she wouldn't do anyone any good if she fell apart. So, she marched back to her car and pulled out her purse. Calling a tow truck, she waited on the road for the truck to arrive.

Minutes ticked by, and the temperature was starting to drop. Finally, the truck arrived. A short man with a thick head of dark hair stepped out of the vehicle. He might be short, but he was built like a Mack truck.

He walked over to the edge of the road. "Looks like you need some help."

"Yes, and you are?" she asked, wondering who Tyrone's Towing had sent.

"Frank Ferrone. Hang on. I'll pull you out of the ditch."

"Sounds wonderful to me."

He got to work hooking a chain up to her car. A short while later, he had pulled her car out of the ditch. He unhooked the chain and had her get in her car and turn the key. It started, thank the Lord.

She tried to pay him.

He held up his hands and backed away. "It's on me."

"Thank you so much for your help." She rubbed her arms. "This is not a place I would want to be stranded."

"No problem, ma'am. You take care. A pretty woman like yourself is vulnerable alone." His dark eyes met hers. "You might want to be more careful in the future. Drive safe now." He climbed into his truck and drove away.

She got in her car and locked the doors.

She was about to leave when suddenly a tow truck pulled up to the curb. A big man stepped out and walked over to her window then knocked. She rolled it down an inch, that was all.

"Can I help you?" she asked.

"I'm here to tow a car out of the ditch, but you're the only car I see." He took off his ballcap and scrubbed his head before slapping it back on and spitting out a stream of chewing tobacco. "Clearly you're not in a ditch."

Her heart started pounding in her chest. She cleared her throat. "Who did you say you were?"

"Tyrone Timmons. I own Tyrone's Towing. I take it you're all set?"

"I'm good, but thanks."

She watched him pull away from the curb and realized she was anything but good. Who was the guy in the truck? And more importantly, what did he want from her? Last she checked, most people didn't do good deeds for no reason these days. Also, this wasn't a road used very often.

Had he been following her?

Shivering, she rolled her window back up all the way. The tow truck headed back the other way. She pulled her car away from the curb, heading toward the coast. The road was dark, and she was the only car for miles. No one came this way unless they lived in one of the houses on the water.

But that didn't stop her from looking in the rearview mirror more often than she wanted to. So when a set of lights appeared behind her, she sped up and turned down the road to Greyson's cottage. She pulled over and waited, her heart pounding in her chest.

The lights never appeared on the road.

She breathed a sigh of relief, and quickly pulled forward and drove the rest of the way, not stopping until she pulled into Greyson's garage and closed the door behind her.

Then she burst into tears.

14

Sparrow calmed herself down. It had been a half hour, and her groceries were going to spoil if she didn't get them in the house soon. No one was going to get her. His cottage was all locked up, and she knew jiu-jitsu. Climbing out of the car, she made several trips inside to unload the groceries.

Turning on her favorite jazz music, she rolled her shoulders to loosen the kinks. She eyed a bottle of rum and felt the old calling. She and the Captain had a long, unhealthy relationship in the past. That's why she kept a bottle around. She needed to know for her own peace of mind that he didn't have a hold over her anymore.

With a deep, cleansing breath, she looked away from the bottle and started storing the groceries in the cupboards, pantry, refrigerator, and freezer. She refused to let her paranoia get the best of her. Maybe the man named Frank had actually just been trying to do a good deed and help her out.

He'd refused to let her pay him, after all.

She went upstairs to her room and changed into purple flannel pajamas and warm fuzzy socks, then she ventured back downstairs into Greyson's master bedroom. He had a massive bedroom suit in dark cherry wood. The four-poster bed was king-size with matching end tables, a long dresser with a trifold mirror, and a tall chest of drawers. His bathroom had a walk-in shower with a rainfall shower head and a separate jacuzzi tub.

The place had definitely been his grandparents'. Greyson was all about the environment. Sparrow was surprised he hadn't changed the humongous shower head to one that conserved water.

Wandering into his walk-in closet, she smiled. This was more like him. There were shelves and racks in a big horseshoe shape, and his clothes didn't even take up one bar. She bet, if she looked, probably half the drawers of the dresser and chest would be empty. Glancing down the row of his clothes, she spotted a black velvet robe.

Her hand moved as if it had a will of its own, and she skimmed her fingertips down the velvety soft material. Slipping it off the hanger, she wrapped herself up in it. Greyson's robe made her feel closer to him, as if he were there hugging her. It was less lonely that way. Heading back out to the kitchen, she realized she was starving. She made herself a chef salad with a thick crust of pumpernickel bread and some hot tea.

She ate in the morning room, looking out over the waves crashing against the shore in the darkness. The moon's light bathed the yard in its romantic silver glow. She could get used to living here with Greyson.

She blinked.

Where had that thought come from?

She was getting way ahead of herself. Who's to say he even felt the same way about her. He had hinted at it for a while, and she had been the one to squash his advances, but maybe all he had wanted was sex. Honestly, she hadn't been with a man since Harlow until Greyson. Maybe that was all she needed.

An affair.

Anything more was terrifying. Thoughts of that could wait. It would be a while before Greyson's body healed anyway. But she had to admit he'd awakened something inside of her, and now being with him was all she could think about. Good Lord, she needed to go to bed and get some sleep.

Clearly, she was delirious.

Finishing her salad, she put her dish in the sink and carried her tea to the living room. She turned the music off and switched on the TV, but the local news channel was talking about Lily's disappearance and what had happened to Sparrow and Greyson. She was in no mood to relive that and not much of a TV person anyway.

She shut the TV off. Sitting there in silence, she finished her tea. She called her mother, but her mother didn't answer. Her sister didn't, either. Maybe she should have taken the men up on their offer of having one of the women stay with her. She could use the company to take her mind off things.

Carrying her teacup to the kitchen, she dug into her small backpack purse she always carried with her for her cellphone. A piece of paper flipped out onto the counter, and Sparrow gasped, dropping her cup. The ceramic teacup hit the tile floor and shattered into hundreds of tiny little shards that flew everywhere.

With shaking hands, Sparrow picked up the note.

BACK OFF, *bitch! Keep your fucking nose out of places it doesn't belong. Quit asking questions and stay out of the northern woods. Go back to where you came from, or your boyfriend is going to wind up dead next time. Tell anyone about this note, and I'll kill you both. You've been warned.*

SPARROW'S HAND SHOOK. Her gaze darted around the house. She ran and checked the doors. The front door was unlocked. How? Greyson wouldn't have left it un-locked, and she had come in through the garage. She quickly locked it, checking it twice this time. She would have to call Buck and have him change the locks.

Had the person come in while she was upstairs changing? Or was the note put in her backpack purse when she was at the hospital? Or the police station? Or the grocery store? Or when she'd gone off the road and Frank Ferrone had helped her?

So many people had access to her bag and could have slipped the note inside.

Her head was reeling with possibilities, which only freaked her out even more. She had finally felt like everything was going to be okay. That had been short lived. Double-checking all the locks in the house, as well as the windows, she turned on all the lights and sat on the couch with a blanket over her, counting down the hours until she could bring Greyson home.

She didn't plan on sleeping a wink.

* * *

THE NEXT MORNING, Greyson awoke after sleeping like the dead.

He hated hospitals. The smell of disinfectant. Doc-tors and nurses probing him at all hours of the night. Needles. He'd been sickly as a child, soas he'd grown older, he'd done everything in his power to stay healthy.

Homeopathic remedies had served him well.

This time, he'd had no choice but to stay the night. The doctors had already checked him out and cleared him to go home. He sat in his hospital bed, waiting for Sparrow to come pick him up. He was itching to leave. All his tests had come back fine. He had fractured ribs and a concussion. No brain bleed or internal bleeding.

Nothing he couldn't heal by himself at home.

Well, not by himself. Sparrow was staying with him. She had been about to say something to him when the bull moose attacked. She hadn't brought it up since. He wondered if it was about their love making. Would things be different now? Would they share a bed? Or would they go back to acting like friends?

He still didn't know what she wanted from him.

Making love to her had been incredible. It had changed him. But that didn't mean it had changed her. He couldn't handle being shot down again, so he was going to stick with his plan to have her make the first move. She would have to be the one to call the shots and ask for what she wanted.

He prayed like hell she wanted him.

There was a knock on his door.

He smiled, looking forward to seeing her face. "Come in."

The door opened...but it wasn't Sparrow.

A man he'd seen around town a couple times before in the past, and recently buying a car from Tommy, stepped inside his room and closed the door behind him. He was of average height and build, with blond hair in need of a trim.

Then again, Greyson couldn't say anything. Look at his own father. The man looked like the Unabomber. And if Greyson were being honest, he wouldn't be at all sure his father hadn't done something criminal.

"Can I help you?" Greyson asked when the man just

stared at him. He felt vulnerable without his gun, and he didn't know this man.

"It's Sparrow," the man said carefully, looking as nervous as Greyson, which made him even more confused.

"What about her?" Greyson set his jaw, an uneasy feeling sweeping over him. How the hell did this guy know his songbird?

"You need to convince her to get as far away from Coldwater Cove as possible. Tell her to go back to Washington."

"Why would she do that?" Greyson asked, adding, "Her career is here." Then the man's words sank in. "And how in the hell do you know she was from Washington?" He watched the man closely.

"Because I was her fiancé."

Greyson's heart slammed against his chest. He felt like he couldn't breathe. If he felt this way, he could only imagine how Sparrow would feel when she found out he was alive and hadn't told her.

"You son of a bitch!" Greyson fisted his hands and tried to stand, then grabbed his ribs and fell back on the bed, groaning.

The man held up his hands in front of him. "Look, man, I'm not trying to cause any trouble. I know what you're thinking, but you would be wrong. I loved her as much as you apparently do. Everything I have done is to protect her."

Greyson gaped at him. "Protect her? You put her through hell. How is *that* protecting her?"

The man's face fell, and Greyson almost believed he still cared. "I can't tell you why."

"Disappearing on her and never coming back is not love. You abandoned her when she needed you most. She didn't deserve that."

"You're right. She didn't deserve that. All I can tell

you is that, if she stays here and keeps going into that section of the woods, she'll be putting herself in danger. Everything I did to try to protect her will have been for nothing."

Greyson narrowed his eyes. "Putting herself in danger from you?"

"No." The man she called Harlow shook his head hard. "I would never hurt her."

Greyson scowled. "Too late for that."

Harlow lifted his regretful gaze. "I mean, I would never *physically* hurt her."

Greyson let out a harsh laugh. "Yeah, well, she lost your baby because of you." He silently cursed. He hadn't meant to reveal that because it wasn't his story to tell. The man made him so angry he forgot himself.

Sparrow would *not* be happy with him.

Harlow's face paled. "Baby?" His voice lowered to barely more than a whisper as he staggered back a step. "She was pregnant when I left?"

"Yes." Greyson let his words sink in. The damage was already done. "She thought you were either eaten by a Grizzly bear or kidnapped."

Harlow's features pinched. "She wouldn't be completely wrong."

"What does that even mean?"

His face went blank once more. "I can't tell you."

"She blamed herself after you vanished without a trace and that nearly destroyed her. She pulled herself together and only came here to be closer to you because you mentioned The Cove once. I can't tell you I can stop her from going into the woods again. Why would I want to, anyway? Do you know something about where Lily is?"

"Look, I had nothing to do with that. I'm not sure where she is. But I do have a proposition for you. I can offer you something you've been searching for, but you have to promise not to tell Sparrow I'm alive, or that we talked."

The man was a fool if he thought Greyson would ever agree to that. "What could you possibly say to ever make me keep something like that from her?"

"I can tell you where your mother is."

* * *

"ARE YOU SURE YOU'RE OKAY?" Sparrow asked Greyson as she settled him into her car outside the hospital. "You look like you've seen a ghost."

He cleared his throat, staring out the window. He hadn't really looked at her since she'd arrived to pick him up. "I'm good," he finally said. "Just ready to go home."

"Me, too. I've had enough drama to last me a lifetime." She closed his door and jogged around to the driver side then slid into the car and started it up, pulling away from the curb, and heading to his house.

Home.

"You and me both," he mumbled, but she heard him.

What was up with him? She was a little worried he was angry with her. Was it because she hadn't said anything about what happened between them? She had meant to, but once again, life had gotten in the way.

"Really, more drama? What happened?" She shot a glance over at him, trying to get him to talk more.

"Nothing," he said quickly and looked at her, then stared back out his window. "I just meant everything we've been through; you know? It's a lot."

"It sure is." She drove in silence for a while. She couldn't tell him about the note because that would put his life in danger, but she decided she could tell him about the rest. She hated secrets.

Nothing good ever came of them.

"I wasn't going to tell you," she said to break the silence, "but I thought I saw Harlow again last night. Right along this stretch of the road. He looked so real, which I know is impossible, but I still swerved to miss him."

"You did?" Greyson stiffened, his head whipping back in her direction and staring at her with wide eyes. "Are you hurt?"

"No, no. I'm okay. I'm sorry. I shouldn't have brought it up." She glanced at him and then back at the road. "I don't want to worry you. You're supposed to be resting, and here I am adding more drama."

"No, it's okay. I want you to tell me everything." She could feel his eyes boring into her. "What happened?"

At least he believed her and didn't think she was crazy. In the past, even her family had thought she was conjuring Harlow's image out of wishful thinking. But even back then, she'd had such a strong sense he was still with her. Now she believed his spirit was with her, watching over her. She just had to find a better way of reacting to it whenever she saw him.

"Well, I ran off the road into the ditch," she admitted. "When I realized I was fine and what had happened to me, I ran up the bank, but there was nothing there."

"That doesn't mean you didn't see what you think you saw." Greyson looked at her so intensely, she didn't know quite what to make of it.

"No, trust me. I've been down that road before. Believing in something I wished so hard for, only to be let down time and again. I can't do that anymore. I know he was just a figment of my imagination."

"I don't know." Greyson shrugged and resumed looking out the window. "I still believe my mom is out there. It doesn't mean that can't be true. Maybe we shouldn't give up hope." He peeked back at her, watching her closely.

She was already shaking her head. "No, I can't live my life that way anymore. I have given everything I have to find out what happened to Harlow. I'm done with that. I have to accept that he's gone, and I may never have the closure I'm looking for." She turned to look at him. "I'm at peace with that because I have you."

Greyson froze, staring at her in the oddest fashion, that suddenly she was worried she'd read his feelings wrong.

She bit her lip and focused on the road again. "I mean, we're living together, temporarily, but it's whatever, you know?"

"Stop." He reached out and held her hand. "It's more than whatever, and we both know it." He sighed. "I just want you to have closure, but selfishly, I want you for myself." He threaded his fingers through hers. "I'm just glad you finally recognize what's between us. No matter what happens, I hope you know I would do anything for you. You're my world, Sparrow. I don't want to live in it without you."

Warmth filled every fiber of her being, and she squeezed his hand. "I'm so happy to hear you say that. I don't want to live without you in mine, either." It felt so good to say that, and she realized she meant every word.

"That being said," he paused until she looked at him, "I think we should let Trent and Hank handle the woods from now on. I can't stand the thought of losing you now that I've found you. Those bad men are still out there. We might not get lucky next time."

"But what about Lily? She was my responsibility, and I blew it. I know you're afraid for me, and I am too after all we've been through, but I can't stand the thought of her out there alone. We have to do something."

"And we will." He kissed her hand. "I promise. Just

not in the woods. We'll investigate in town and see what we find."

"Okay, for you." She looked at him as she added, "But just so you know, if that doesn't pan out, I'm going to find her no matter how long I have to look or what I have to do."

15

Sparrow headed into town after getting Greyson settled. Buck was there, changing the locks and installing a security system. Since Greyson had someone with him, she decided to stop by her office. Greyson had assured her he didn't need a babysitter. He was a little bumped and bruised, but he wasn't broken. Besides, Sparrow couldn't just sit around, staring at the ocean and doing nothing.

Not after that note.

That note proved Lily hadn't been eaten by a wild animal. Something was going on in those woods, and someone was working very hard to keep her from finding out what. Sparrow had to believe Lily was still alive. She couldn't live with herself otherwise. She had to try to find her, but she'd promised Greyson she wouldn't go back into the woods. That she would look in town, so that's what she planned to do.

For now.

She pulled her car into the parking lot of the conservation office and cut the engine. She sat there for a minute, just staring at the building. After taking a deep breath, she went inside. Victoria sat at her desk, talking to Christopher, with papers and maps spread out on the table between them and half-filled Styrofoam coffee cups.

Longing to get back to work and do what she loved hit Sparrow hard.

They both stopped talking and stared at Sparrow with raised eyebrows.

"What are you doing here?" Victoria secured her silver hair in a ponytail and stared at her with confusion.

"I'm just checking in. That's all, I promise." Sparrow shrugged. "I just can't sit back and do nothing with Lily still out there." She looked at Chris. "Have you found anything more at the field site?"

He shook his head and pushed his glasses up his nose. "We've made some good progress on restoring the habitat, though, despite some crazy naturalists. This year's group is led by a man named Nigel."

"I've heard about him," Sparrow said, nodding. "Greyson told me Nigel and some hunter named Greggor got into it at the gun club, and then later at The Claw. They were butting heads over birdwatching and hunting in the same area."

"That is why we work together with the rangers." Victoria blew out a frustrated breath and threw her hands up. "There are set places for each of those groups to be so that everyone will remain safe."

"That man is obsessed." Chris scoffed. "He's determined to get a sighting of several birds on his list, no matter the cost. I told them spotting a few of those species would be a longshot. He didn't listen. In fact, he actually gave me attitude when I told him he had to leave. He was risking jeopardizing our research by being in our site area."

"I'll have to talk to Wanda about better enforcement

of the woods." Victoria set her jaw as she made a note on a pad of paper.

"Good idea." Chris ran a hand over his bald head. "Nigel isn't the only problem we've encountered."

"What do you mean?" Sparrow asked, wondering if there was something wrong with the research.

Chris cleaned his glasses then put them back on his nose as he looked her in the eye. "We had a run-in with Conservation Consultants again."

Sparrow frowned. Just when she thought she might have been overreacting, they turned around and started acting suspicious again. "Ozzy and Peter? What kind of run-in? The last time I saw them during the search for Lily, they told me they were working a new field site."

"Exactly." Chris snapped his fingers. "They should have no need to venture into our field area. I told them as much, and they claimed they were just checking on our site. Then they asked if there was any progress on finding Lily."

"Did you believe them?" Victoria asked.

He shook his head. "Frankly, I believe they thought no one was working on the site. They seemed surprised to see me and my team arrive."

"Did they tell you what kind of work they're doing for their client, or who their client is?" Sparrow asked. "They told me it was confidential."

"Same here." Chris nodded. "They seemed harmless enough, just a little secretive. But you know how that goes when it comes to private labs."

"That's true," Victoria chimed in. "This isn't the first time the state has had problems with private labs and what their clients ask them to do. Keep your eyes open and report to me if anything else happens. Be safe out there, Chris. Stay around the field area only. I know we're pressed for time and have a lot to do before winter, but I don't need any other teams getting hurt or disappearing."

Chris nodded.

"I really am so sorry. Lily was my responsibility. This is all my fault." Sparrow wrapped her arms around her middle, still feeling the heavy weight of her assistant going missing on her watch.

"I'm not blaming you, Sparrow." Victoria squeezed her shoulder. "No one is. That's not the reason you got suspended." She leveled a serious stare at Sparrow. "Taking a company vehicle to venture off on your own and putting yourself in danger was reckless. I won't have that from my employees."

"I know. It won't happen again."

Victoria patted her arm. "I know it won't. Give yourself some time to heal. I need you back healthy and ready to work."

"But my scrapes and bruises aren't bad."

"I'm talking emotionally, Sparrow." Victoria's eyes and tone gentled. "You need both a healthy mind and body to be successful in field work. You've been through a lot lately. Greyson, too. Wanda's on the same page as me. She doesn't want him in the field any more than I want you there."

"You can't really compare us. I mean, he's much worse off than I am," Sparrow's voice trailed off at Victoria's firm look, so Sparrow added, "but I hear you loud and clear. No field work. I will stay in town and keep out of harm's way." Victoria didn't need to see the fingers crossed behind Sparrow's back.

"Good." Victoria nodded once, sharply. "Now go get some rest and take care of yourself. I'll be putting you back to work soon."

Sparrow waved and left the office, feeling frustrated. Every day that went by without them finding

Lily made her chances of coming home alive slim to none.

* * *

"Thanks, Buck, I appreciate it. This will make me feel a lot safer." Greyson tested the new locks the man had installed.

Buck was new to town, and Larry had taken him under his wing, but he hadn't made many friends yet. Larry had tried to get him to go to the pub to meet the guys, but he said Buck was shy. Larry had hooked him up with Tia to find a better place than the hotel for him to stay, but Greyson didn't know much else about him.

Buck nodded once and handed him a manual, shifting his feet awkwardly and not quite meeting his eyes. "Security system is the newest in the line. Larry told me to go with that. Hope that's okay."

"It's perfect. I want the best so Sparrow will feel safe."

Buck's eyes met Greyson's and held at the mention of Sparrow. "I don't blame you. It's a scary world out there, even scarier when you care about people." He looked around. "Nice house." Then he looked away. "Gotta go. Ms. Johnson's showing me a town house today." He picked up his toolkit and stepped outside the front door, already heading to his truck at a quick pace.

"Thanks again," Greyson hollered after him, closing and locking the door behind him and turning on the security system.

The man was a little socially awkward, but he did good work. That was all Greyson cared about at the moment. Despite his concussion and cracked ribs, everything else on him worked just fine. He wandered around his kitchen, looking in cupboards and the refrigerator, taking stock of the groceries Sparrow had bought.

He knew from what she'd told him that she couldn't cook worth a damn.

He chuckled, thinking dinners might be his chore if he wanted to survive. He loved to cook but didn't get to nearly enough for his liking when he was in the field. He'd been on his own for so long, in a job that he loved but didn't pay well, considering the danger involved. He didn't want to waste money eating out every night, but certain times of the year, when activity in the woods was busy, he didn't always have a choice.

Even though his grandparents occasionally tried to give him money, he refused to take it. It was enough he was living in the *cottage* rent-free. He was determined to pay for everything else on his own. Now that he had some downtime, he figured tonight was as good as any to start cooking. Besides, he was already bored. He'd never survive mandatory time off when the woods were mysteriously dangerous, and Lily was still missing.

Turning on some seventy's folk music, Greyson called in a favor from Jack and had him drop off the ingredients for seared scallops and mushroom risotto with chocolate truffles for dessert. Jack was between shifts at The Claw, so he didn't mind. And Greyson trusted Jack the most to pick out the best ingredients.

Greyson didn't want Sparrow to know what he was up to. He really wanted to impress her and thank her for all that she had done to save his life in the woods. She was incredible. He would not have survived without her. He owed her everything.

But his guilt was eating him alive.

He wanted to tell her about Harlow paying him a visit at the hospital, but if he did that, then he would never know the truth about what had happened to his mother. The deal was that Greyson would keep Sparrow out of the woods, and then, when the time was right, Harlow would tell Greyson everything he knew.

At first Greyson didn't believe him.

The man could be making the whole thing up. It wasn't like the scandal of Greyson's mother going missing and his father being a suspect five years ago was a secret. All the man had to do was Google his name, and all the sordid details were there.

But when Harlow mentioned his mother's mono-grammed handkerchief, he could no longer deny the man knew something. That was the same handkerchief his mother had on her the day she went missing. Greyson had made it for her when he was in middle school, and his mother had always kept it with her, saying it was her good luck charm.

Apparently, it wasn't so lucky because he'd never seen her again.

Greyson owed Sparrow. He'd like to think that keeping Harlow's reappearance from her was for her own protection, at least for now, but he needed to know what had happened to his mother. He needed to know if she was dead or alive. He needed to clear his father's name. They needed closure. He knew Sparrow needed closure, too, and he would give that to her just as soon as he could. But for now, he would keep his silence and try to make it up to her in other ways.

A knock on the door sounded.

Walking across the room, Greyson peeked out the peephole and saw Jack. He opened the door with a grin. "You're a life saver, man."

"You can pay me back by making this for me some-time." Jack carried the grocery bags over to the kitchen counter. "All this time I've been feeding you, I had no idea you could cook. Sparrow's going to love this."

"I hope so. What do I owe you?"

Jack held his hands up. "It's on me, brother. Anything to help your sorry ass land a good woman like Sparrow. The girls all love her."

Greyson's heart warmed just hearing her name. "She is pretty special, but she's been through a lot."

"So have you, buddy." Jack lightly squeezed Greyson's shoulder. "You need anything at all you let me know. Okay?"

"Will do. And thanks, man. I appreciate it."

"Anytime." Jack headed for the door. "Let me know how it comes out."

Greyson nodded as Jack let himself out, then he got to work.

He started with the chocolate truffles. Heating cream and chocolate, he melted them together and then froze the mixture while he did other things. When it was ready, he rolled the balls in chopped pistachios that he refrigerated for later.

Moving on to the meal, he cut up some mushrooms, garlic, shallots, and chives. He sauteed them in olive oil, then added the rice. He added the demi-glaze and water next, followed by the crème fraiche, butter, Verjus, and the cooked vegetables with truffle zest. Next up, he seared the scallops and placed them on top of the risotto then garnished the dish with crispy onions and sliced chives.

The rich flavors filled the air as Sparrow finally got home.

He'd set the table with his mother's fine china, candles, sparkling water, the food, and the dessert. She would be so proud of him. He took after her with her love of cooking. He only hoped Sparrow would be as pleased.

Sparrow called his name and knocked when she couldn't get in.

He walked over and let her in, wearing a wide smile he couldn't keep off his face if he tried.

She laughed. "What's that smile for?" Before he could answer, she inhaled deeply and pushed past him. "What smells amazing?"

The look on her face was worth everything.

She peeked up at him. "You did all this for me?"

"Yes."

"But I'm supposed to be taking care of you." She held a pizza in her hands and looked down sheepishly.

He took it from her. "We'll have that tomorrow for lunch." He set it on the counter as she took her coat off. "Tonight, I want to take care of you."

"But I'm fine."

"So am I, really. I can look after myself, and I love to cook." He pulled out her seat and gestured for her to sit. "This was my mother's recipe. I wanted to do something to thank you for saving my life."

"You saved mine as well." She reached out and took his hand.

He gave hers a gentle squeeze. "I'm beginning to think we saved each other in more ways than one."

She flushed pink, pulling her hand back, and looked at the food as if still a little uncomfortable with moving on from a man she thought was dead. Greyson wanted to tell her she didn't owe Harlow anything after everything he'd done to her, but he couldn't.

"Eat up," he said instead.

"It looks wonderful," she said in awe.

He took his seat. "Let's hope it tastes as good as it looks."

She filled her fork with the food, put it in her mouth, then her eyes rolled back as if she were in heaven. "This is incredible."

"You're incredible." He raised his glass.

She raised hers and said shyly, "So are you."

"To new beginnings," he said with hope in his voice.

"Cheers to that," she said with a sweet smile.

They clinked glasses and sipped in a promising toast, but Greyson's stomach filled with dread. He was finally getting everything he hadn't realized he'd wanted or needed, and one realization hit him hard.

She was going to hate him when she learned the truth.

16

———

OVER THE NEXT WEEK, Sparrow stayed out of the woods like Greyson had asked her to. They'd questioned everyone they could think of: Lily's friends, her family, people who might not like her, and even her ex-boyfriends.

Everyone seemed to have an alibi for their whereabouts on the night Lily was taken. They started looking at people Lily didn't know who she might have stumbled across in the woods, doing something they shouldn't be.

Sparrow didn't trust Ozzy and Peter nosing around different sites still, even after being warned not to. They obviously were interested in something in that particular area. Then there was Greggor's hunting group. They'd ventured into areas other than their designated one, in hopes of bagging a big buck.

Maybe they were shooting more than their hunting license allowed and she'd caught them. And Nigel's group had made it clear they would stop at nothing to get the coveted bird sightings they wanted. Maybe Lily had caught them doing something illegal to sabotage the hunters.

And then there was the wild man.

Sparrow still couldn't believe he was Greyson's father, Mason. The man left five years ago. Poor Greyson had no idea his father had been hiding out in the woods the whole time. He'd been very secretive, saying he couldn't disclose his mission yet.

What if Lily had stumbled upon what he was doing?

The man seemed a little unstable. He might have been desperate enough to keep his secret that he took her to keep her quiet. Whoever it was hadn't made any ransom demands, yet no one had found her, either.

That gave Sparrow hope that her friend was still alive.

Sparrow pulled into The Lost Horizon to meet up with the girls for lunch. She loved living with Greyson, and they had been hinting at wanting something more. She hadn't felt these feelings in a long time, and even with all the drama, she hadn't had a drink. Whatever *something more* was, it hovered in the air, surrounding them with a cloud of hope.

It had been difficult for her to let down her guard and risk getting hurt again, but with Greyson, it felt different. Safe. *Right*. He was so kind and gentle with her, letting her be the one to take the lead. They had kissed a lot and slept in the same bed every night, but they hadn't made love again.

The first time had been a *thank-God-we're-still-alive* moment.

It had been intense and passionate and fast, leaving her wanting more. She craved his touch like she craved air after nearly drowning, but she didn't want to hurt him. She'd said as much, but he had assured her he could handle any pain if it meant being with her again. He said he would wait until she was ready. Ready for what, exactly, was the question.

They both knew what happened between them was a lot more than just sex.

She bit her bottom lip as she smiled. She was ready. He might cook orgasmic dinners, but she knew a thing or two about sinful, delectable desserts. She had special plans to surprise him later with pleasure, not pain, that very night. There were other ways, slow and gentle ways, and she intended to show him every single one.

But first, she had a lunch date with her ladies, and then some shopping to do.

Sparrow opened the door to the restaurant and took a quick step back. "Not this time." She laughed and held the door open for Abe the hunter, who was just leaving.

He skidded to a stop with surprised eyes and then laughed a deep, hearty laugh and bowed his salt and pepper buzzed head. "Good to *not* run into you again, Sparrow." He winked and shot her a smile that never failed to brighten her day whenever she ran into him.

"Well, what's the verdict? Any luck with the hunt?" She liked Abe. She didn't really like hunting, but she knew it was a necessity to prevent overpopulation and starvation for the wild herds.

He sighed. "Not yet. I've gotten close a couple times, but no luck yet. No worries. I'm not a quitter. My late wife used to say I was a stubborn mule, but more times than not, my stubbornness has paid off."

"Oh, I'm so sorry about your loss." Her hand fluttered over her chest. "I know a little something about loss."

"Well, thank you for that. Sorry for your own loss. It really does get easier with time." He nodded. "Mine was a long time ago. Died during childbirth, but at least I have a part of her that will live on forever in my son." He patted her arm. "You're a good girl, Sparrow. Do you have any children?"

Her heart dropped to her stomach. "No, unfortunately, I don't. That was part of my loss." She blinked, surprised she'd revealed that much. She usually didn't talk about that, but Abe had shared his own loss, and maybe he was right. Maybe things were finally getting easier for her, and it was time to move on.

His eyes widened. "I'm so sorry. I truly believe we will see our loved ones again someday. You take care of yourself, now."

"I will. Same to you. I'll be crossing my fingers you score big this time."

"I'll take it. I can use all the help I can get." He waved as he walked away.

Sparrow headed into the restaurant, feeling better about her plans this evening with Greyson. Now more than ever she truly believed it really was time for her to move on. The girls were right. Coldwater Cove would give her what she needed and already felt like home...

And Greyson had stolen her heart.

Sparrow spotted the girls almost immediately. She walked toward their table when she saw Tommy sitting with Buck. She waved to the maintenance man, and he waved back then looked at the table her friends sat at and blushed three shades of red. Tommy glanced in her direction curiously, then arched a brow and waved, looking confused. He glanced over at their table briefly before turning back to Buck.

Sparrow could relate. What the heck was up with Buck?

Sparrow joined Laura, Stacy, Olivia, Zoe, and Tia at their usual table. "Hi, ladies. I'm so glad to see you all."

"We're thrilled to see you alive and well after the scares you've been giving us lately," Stacy said. "I know I asked for excitement from you girls, but I could do without this kind."

"Same here." Olivia tucked her silky black hair behind her ear. "I think I've aged ten years in the past few weeks."

"Well, I think I've put on five pounds from eating and drinking away my stress." Zoe rubbed her belly. "Jack keeps feeding me because I'm working so much, while Trent and Hank keep asking me for beers to compare notes."

"The woods are a mess for sure." Sparrow took a calming breath. "Greyson can't sit still. He's worried over what's happening, yet he won't let either of us go into the woods and do our part. I know he's worried, but it seems like there's more to it than that. I don't know. I give up trying to figure him out."

"You and me both." Laura looked in Tommy's direction. "Every time I try to schedule time with my husband, he backs out. He complains when I don't spend enough time with him, yet, when I jump through hoops to make it happen, he cancels for a business meeting." She gestured towards the table where he and Buck sat. "It's like he's punishing me for being successful."

"I'm so sorry, honey." Stacy shook her head. "We need to make our lunch date a night out. I think we could all use one."

"Amen to that." Laura sighed. "Tommy and I were supposed to meet here a half hour before my lunch date with you girls for appetizers. Then suddenly he has to meet with Buck at that exact same time. Apparently, his mechanic just quit, and he has issues in his showroom that need fixing. I get that. He has a lot of inventory he needs to sell, but did he have to schedule this meeting during our brief lunch date? I don't know what to do anymore. We used to be the IT couple."

"Marriage is hard," Stacy said. "It definitely takes work. And children only make it even more difficult to find enough time for each other. Trent has been acting strangely, himself. I keep catching him on the phone, but when I ask him who he's talking to, he makes up some excuse. I don't think he's lying to me, but he's definitely not telling me the whole truth."

"Well, now you guys are scaring me. I have news, but now I'm terrified to tell you all." Olivia looked at each one of them and then thrust out her hand. "Hank asked me to marry him, and I said yes."

They all squealed, oohing and ahhing over the rock on her finger.

"That's wonderful news," Tia said. "I'd just be happy to find a boyfriend. There are no good prospects in town who are single. Or the ones that are single who make a move on me are bad boys."

"You're a strong ass woman," Zoe said. "Why don't you make a move first? I see the way Buck looks at you. He's a handsome man, he's just a little shy and awkward."

Tia's jaw fell open. "You think Buck likes me? I always thought he was handsome, but then he barely speaks to me."

"Duh. Literally everyone in town can see it but you." Zoe looked at the other women. "Am I right, ladies?"

They all nodded except Sparrow.

"Clearly I missed the memo," Sparrow said, "but that makes sense now that I think about it. And that would explain the look he gave toward Tia when I walked in."

"Really?" Tia looked in his direction. He made eye contact, blushed, then quickly looked away. "I had no idea. All this time I've been working with him to find him a place to call home, and I just thought he was a shy introvert, but I'm outgoing enough for the both of us." She studied him more closely. "He most definitely has potential."

"How about this? If you ask him out, I'll finally tell Jack I want him to ask me to move in with him." Zoe blew out a frustrated breath. "I mean, I'm there all the time anyway. You would think it would be a no brainer. Men can be so clueless sometimes."

They finished their lunch, talking about various things, but Sparrow couldn't stop thinking about the women talking about being brave enough to ask for what they wanted. That just solidified her plans for this evening. They said their goodbyes, and she headed out the door with a renewed sense of purpose.

She was going to seduce Greyson tonight.

She picked up a special outfit that made her feel alive again. Sparkling, non-alcoholic champagne and chocolate covered strawberries made their way into her cart. Scented candles that smelled like a rainforest on a lush tropical island were her next purchase. Then, as much as he loved to cook and she appreciated his efforts, she wanted to spoil him for a change.

Sparrow loved The Claw for seafood. But Betty Clark made the best homemade spaghetti and meatballs with Italian bread at the Lost Horizon. After picking up that, Sparrow headed back toward Greyson's house.

The Lost Horizon was on the edge of town inland near the woods. It wasn't that far from their offices and park trails people walked and ran on. Sparrow had almost passed that when she spotted Greyson's car. She frowned. What was he doing heading toward his office? He wasn't supposed to go near the woods any more than she was.

Going on gut instinct, she turned away from her destination and followed him.

Keeping far enough away that he wouldn't spot her, she watched him pass the office. He went a little further down the road to a spot that was secluded. A pull-off on the side of the road for hunters to park and enter state land.

What was he doing?

He just sat there, waiting. This was ridiculous. Her gut had never steered her wrong before, but maybe it was playing tricks on her now. She was about to pull off the road behind him, when a man walked out of the woods.

Sparrow stepped on her breaks and jerked to a stop just out of view of the men. She squinted harder to see better and then gasped. It couldn't be. The man she had been seeing in her visions wasn't a vision at all. But how was that possible? Harlow Rigsby was standing there, plain as day, talking to Greyson Adler. Her heartbeat started to pound in her ears as questions hammered her brain...

Harlow was alive?

Harlow was in Coldwater Cove?

Greyson knew Harlow?

And neither one of them had thought to tell her any of this. So many emotions warred within her. Hope, happiness, confusion, despair, anger. All she knew at the moment was that she didn't want to see either one of them ever again.

Apparently, Greyson's father wasn't the only one keeping secrets.

* * *

GREYSON HAD DECIDED to come clean with Sparrow.

It would kill him not learning about what had happened to his mother, but he couldn't bear losing Sparrow over not telling her that her ex-fiancé was still alive. He hadn't told her yet, but he was in love with her. Living together had only confirmed the crazy connection between them wasn't just in his head. It was real and worth fighting for.

He planned to tell her tonight, but first he had to let Harlow know the deal was off. Greyson got out of his jeep when he saw the blond man exit the woods. Harlow looked left then right before approaching the vehicle.

"What's up?" Harlow asked. "It's dangerous meeting in public. What were you thinking?"

"I needed to talk to you." Greyson stepped forward and lowered his voice. "It's important, or I wouldn't be here."

"What could possibly be that important for you to risk calling me out?" Harlow balled his fists. "I told you I would be in touch when the time was right."

Greyson stood up straight, using his tall height and muscular frame to his advantage. In his state, he couldn't afford to get in a fistfight. But he also couldn't afford to back down. "That's not going to work for me now."

Harlow clenched his jaw. "What's changed?"

"Sparrow." Greyson stared at him, silently daring him to say anything.

Harlow's face paled, and he relaxed his fists, his shoulders slumping slightly. "What about Sparrow?"

Greyson stood at ease. The man clearly still cared about her. "She deserves to know the truth."

"You really don't get it." Harlow shook his head. "Everything I have ever done is to protect her."

Greyson puckered his brow. They obviously wanted the same thing so why wouldn't he come clean with what was going on. "From what? From whom?"

Harlow set his jaw. "I told you I can't tell you."

"I've heard that one too many times lately, and I'm over it." Greyson grunted. "No more secrets. Either you tell her, or I will."

"If you tell her, then you'll never hear the truth about your mother."

"That's a risk I have to take. She needs closure." Greyson stabbed his finger in Harlow's direction. "You owe her that much. If you really love her the way you say you do, and you know you can't be with her for her own safety, then you should want her to be happy." Greyson shoved a hand through his hair and began to pace. "She can't move on if you won't let her, dude. You have her thinking she's losing her mind by appearing in front of her in random places. You seriously need to stop that."

"I was trying to mess with her head so she would leave. I hate it." Harlow's face twisted in pain. "I didn't know about the baby, I swear, though it wouldn't have made a difference. My hands are tied." He looked Greyson in the eyes. "I'm telling you it's not safe for her out there." His face took on genuine worry. "You need to try harder to convince her not to go in the woods."

"I did and she hasn't, but what we're doing is not right, and I can't be a part of it anymore. No matter how much closure I might want, or my father might need, it's not fair to Sparrow." Greyson let out a sigh and muttered beneath his breath, "He'll just have to stay in the woods until he gets over her."

"Wait...your father is the wild man in the woods that everyone is talking about?" Harlow gaped at him, obviously having overheard him. He shook his head over and over, backing away towards the woods. "That's not good."

A bad feeling swept through Greyson. Harlow knew about his old man? For the first time, Greyson was worried. "What do you mean, that's not good?"

A car engine sounded in the distance, and they both looked around but didn't see anything.

"It's not safe here. I have to go." Harlow locked eyes with Greyson. "This changes everything."

"THANKS FOR LETTING me crash at your place tonight," Sparrow said to Zoe.

She'd seen more than she could handle of Greyson and Harlow and had headed straight home, throwing her dinner and negligee in the trash. She'd packed an overnight bag and headed straight to Coldwater Commons, not leaving him a note, or answering his calls.

The hotel had been full because of the festival goers, hunters, and birdwatchers, so she'd sat there in the parking lot, letting her anger and disillusionment fuel her. Then she remembered Zoe saying she still had her apartment, even though she rarely stayed there.

All it took was one phone call, and Zoe had dropped everything, coming to her rescue.

"Hey, girl, that's what friends are for." Zoe set a large pizza on her kitchen table between them by a pile of napkins and pulled a couple plates from her cupboard. She handed one to Sparrow. "Besides, I figure some time apart from Jack might make him realize what he's missing if I'm not there on a more permanent basis." She pulled out a beer from the refrigerator for herself and arched a brow. "Something to drink?"

"Soda?"

Grabbing a cola and a glass of ice, she handed them to Sparrow then sat down to grab a slice of the thick sausage and mushroom pie and took a bite.

"Thank you." Sparrow popped the tab and poured the fizzy drink in her glass. "For everything."

"Well, thank you, too. I love girls' night." Zoe winked. "You should have seen Jack's face when I ordered a large pizza from The Claw then picked it up and left without a word. He gave me a puzzled look, but all I did was smile at him and blow him a kiss, then wave my fingers as I walked out the door."

Sparrow puckered her brow, worrying that she might be stirring up trouble for them. "I'm sure he's wondering who you're sharing it with and where. Are you sure this is okay?" She took a bite of her pizza, starving.

It had been a long, emotional day.

"Let him wonder. It's all good, I promise." Zoe raised her beer and took a swig. She still hadn't talked to Jack like she said she would because she still wasn't sure she wanted to. "We need a little excitement in our lives. That boy is getting way too comfortable. Maybe this will make him step up his game. But enough about me and Jack. What's going on with you and Greyson?"

"Nothing." Sparrow set her jaw. "Not anymore, at least." She raised her gaze to Zoe's. "I didn't tell you girls yet, but I was engaged once. A couple years ago."

Zoe's eyes widened. "What happened?"

"He was a wildlife biologist like me. We were working in the field together back in Washington, when a Grizzly attacked. I did everything wrong and ran away. The bear was about to give chase, but Harlow distracted it, and it chased him deeper into the woods. I never saw or heard from him again."

"Oh no, that's horrible."

"It gets worse." Sparrow inhaled a deep breath. "I

found out I was pregnant, but I was so distraught over my fiancé going missing, I lost the baby."

Zoe reached out and squeezed her hand. "Honey, I'm so sorry."

"I spiraled downward into a horrible place, using alcohol to numb the pain. Through therapy and the help of my family, I pulled myself out of my depression and started over. I took the job in Coldwater Cove because Harlow had mentioned it one time, and it made me feel closer to him."

"I can relate," Zoe said softly.

Sparrow blinked back tears. "What happened?"

"I was never pregnant, but I did lose someone I loved. My fiancé and I were in the Coast Guard together when our ship went down. I too did everything wrong and lost him. I blamed myself for a long time, but Jack helped me see it wasn't my fault. I deserved to be happy and find love again."

"That's wonderful. The hardest part for me was not knowing what happened to Harlow and if he was dead or alive. Greyson was like Jack. He helped me realize I couldn't stop living. I was so excited to show him just how much he means to me earlier today. I planned a whole evening. Dinner. Dessert." She wiped her tears away and sat up straighter. "But after what happened, I don't care to ever see him again."

"I don't understand. Everyone can see how much you both care about each other. What could possibly have happened to change your feelings towards him?"

"Seeing Harlow and Greyson talking together by the woods. They looked way too chummy for a casual run-in."

"What?" Zoe gaped at her. "I thought Harlow was missing?"

"So did I, and that's the problem. Greyson obviously knew Harlow was not only alive but in Coldwater

Cove. I've been seeing Harlow at random places since I've been here, but I thought I was losing my mind. Greyson knew that." She shook her head. "They've both played me for a fool."

"Did you confront them?"

"I couldn't. I wanted to, but I froze. I was in a state of shock and couldn't process what I was seeing. I just needed to get out of there."

"What are you going to do?"

"I know what I'm *not* going to do. I'm not going to listen to Greyson telling me to stay out of the woods because they're dangerous. Now I know he was just worried about me finding Harlow." Sparrow shook her head and choked back sobs. "I have no idea what Harlow was thinking. I've mourned him for two years and lost our baby because of my guilt over what happened to him. To find out nothing happened to him, yet he let me believe he was dead, is more hurtful than anything. Did he really want away from me that badly?"

"Do you think he had anything to do with those men who shot at you and Greyson?" Zoe asked.

"I don't know who he is anymore. I thought I knew who Greyson was, but it turns out I don't know either of them."

"They always say that truth is crazier than fiction." Zoe shook her head, looking amazed. "It makes you wonder how well you can really know someone. It certainly doesn't sound like the Greyson I know."

"Yeah, well, there's more you don't know about him." Sparrow decided she didn't owe him any more loyalty, and maybe it would help her find Lily, so what did she have to lose?

"What's that?"

"The wild man in the woods is Greyson's long-lost father, Mason Adler."

"I need to tell Trent and Hank this." Zoe called Trent first and put him on speaker.

"What's up, Zoe? It must be important if you're calling me during the after-dinner witching hour with baby Lizzie." The baby screamed non-stop in the background. Suddenly, the sound of a vacuum came on. "Thanks, Stacy. I'll be right back." They heard him walk into another room and shut the door. "Okay, shoot. I only have a minute."

"I have breaking news," Zoe said. "Greyson's father, Mason, is alive and in the woods. He's the wild man who everyone has been talking about."

There was a pause on the line.

Zoe frowned at Sparrow.

Trent sighed. "I know."

"You know?" Zoe blurted.

"He's the informant I've been working with."

"For how long?" Sparrow interjected.

"Is that Sparrow?"

"Yes, Sheriff."

"Greyson has been looking all over for you. He's worried sick."

"He deserves to be."

He paused a beat. "You two have a fight?"

"I just needed some time to myself. I'm at Zoe's. Tell him I'm fine, but not to bother me. I'll talk to him when I'm ready."

"Will do. Whatever it is, I hope you two work things out."

"Back to Greyson's father." Sparrow cleared her throat. "He told me his mother went missing five years ago and then his father left town when the case went cold. Greyson didn't know where he was until we ran into him in the woods. Mason said he couldn't come into town and help find Lily because he was working on something."

"That's right," Trent said. "I discovered him right after I became sheriff. I knew of the cold case surrounding his wife's disappearance and that there wasn't enough evidence to hold him. He's a free man, he just chooses to remain estranged from everyone. He asked that I not tell his son where he was. He didn't want to come home until he had answers for them both about his wife. I agreed to keep his silence if he agreed to be my eyes and ears in the woods."

"And what has he found?" Zoe asked.

"A lot. I don't know all the details yet, but just know this." A pause filled the line. "Something big is about to go down tomorrow. I'll fill you in when I know more."

"Roger that," Zoe said.

"And Sparrow?" Trent added.

"Yes?"

"Stay out of the woods. They're dangerous." Then he hung up.

* * *

GREYSON SAT at the bar in The Claw, sipping coffee with Trent and Hank. They preferred breakfast with Jack to eating at the Lost Horizon like most, so Greyson had purposely joined them there. The pub was quiet this time of day, and he needed answers.

He couldn't believe Sparrow had left him.

He didn't understand what had happened, and she didn't leave a note. She wasn't taking his calls or texts, either. He'd found the dinner and negligee in the trash. She'd obviously been planning a special night, so what had happened between lunch and dinner to make her want to leave him?

After everything they had been through together.

"Did you know she was going to stay with Zoe?" Greyson asked Jack.

"No." Jack rubbed his jaw. "I thought it was strange when Zoe ordered a large pizza and then left. She usually eats with me and spends the night. I sent her a text, but she didn't answer me, either. Kinda had me worried, like she was mad at me about something. I know now that Sparrow spent the night with her, but I still think something is off with Zoe."

"Better find out what before it's too late." Greyson took another sip of his black coffee. "I just don't know what the hell I did." He looked at Trent. "Did she say anything other than she was safe and not ready to talk?"

"She told me about your father being the wild man," Trent said and looked at Hank. "I had to come clean about him being my informant."

"What? My father is your informant?" Greyson was stunned. He felt better that his father wasn't involved in something illegal. He was actually working with the police to try to stop whatever was happening out there. If only he had trusted Greyson to handle it, he would have worked with him side-by-side.

"Informant? Wait, Mason Adler is the wild man? Why didn't you tell me?" Hank raised a brow. "I knew there was something up. I haven't been here that long, but I could tell you were getting more secretive and taking a lot of phone calls."

"I couldn't tell anyone. I found him right after I became Sheriff, and we made a deal. Lately, this deal is finally paying off." Trent looked at each of them. "Something big is going down in the woods today. I've been making preparations. Once Mason gives me the final details, we'll move in."

"Just say the word, and I'll be ready," Hank said.

The door to The Claw flew open, and Zoe stormed inside with a serious look on her face. She glanced at Greyson, then turned to Trent and Hank. "She's gone."

"Who?" Trent asked.

"Sparrow. She took her things and left."

"Maybe she went back to our place?" Greyson stood.

Zoe was already shaking her head. "I checked. She's not there. She's not at the hotel or with any of the girls, either."

"I told her to stay out of the woods," Trent said.

Greyson shook his head. "She doesn't much care for people telling her that."

"Why would she go into the woods?" Hank asked.

Zoe looked at Greyson. "To find her fiancé."

Greyson's eyes widened. "Oh, God. She saw us, didn't she? That's why she ran away."

"What is going on?" Trent asked.

"Sparrow's fiancé, Harlow, went missing two years ago. She started over in The Cove because he mentioned it one time." Zoe glared at Greyson. "Then she saw the two of you talking by the woods yesterday morning. You knew she thought she was losing her mind, having visions of him. You knew she needed closure, yet you said nothing of having met him. Why would you do that?"

"Looks like Trent and Mason aren't the only ones keeping secrets," Hank said. "Spill it, Adler."

"Harlow showed up at the hospital and confessed who he was. He made me promise to keep Sparrow out of the woods and not tell her he was alive and in The Cove." Greyson looked at Trent. "I only agreed because he said he knew where my mother was."

Hank rubbed the back of his neck. "This story just gets crazier by the minute."

Greyson looked at Zoe. "I only met with Harlow to tell him the deal was off. That Sparrow deserved to know the truth even if it meant I would never learn the truth about my mother."

"Don't be so sure about that," Trent said. "I just got a text." He looked at them all. "It's time to move."

* * *

DAMMIT! I mentally cursed, as I paced around the area. I kicked an item on the floor and threw another across the room. Anger and frustration boiled within me. I fucking deserved everything that was coming to me. It wasn't fair.

It was my turn to get what I wanted for a change.

"Who's there?" Lily asked, startling me. I'd forgotten she was there for a moment. She sat against the wall with her knees drawn to her chest. "Please let me go."

I wanted to say something, but I couldn't risk her knowing who I was. I wasn't a monster. I tried to make sure she was comfortable and gave her the food she liked. I didn't have anything personal against her. I just deserved some recognition for everything I did.

I was through with other people stealing the spotlight from me.

"Just talk to me. I need to hear another human voice." Lily started to cry.

I hated when a woman cried, so I hesitated for a moment, but shook off the temptation to come clean. I didn't want to have to kill her. Looking around the area, I had a lot of valuable things I didn't want to lose. But I wasn't about to go down with the others if we got caught. I regretted getting involved with such fuckups. I glanced one last time at Lily sobbing on the floor, and I walked up the stairs, closing the door behind me without a single glance back.

If I had to, I would destroy the evidence along with all loose ends inside.

SPARROW STILL HAD the maps Greyson had given her for her field work. He was very thorough and had given her a much broader map in case anything ever happened, and she needed it. At the time she had thought he was a bit over the top, but now she appreciated his eagle-scout-level attention to detail. The man was always prepared.

She wasn't about to stay out of the woods.

If something was going down, then Lily was in jeopardy. Sparrow had to at least try to save her before it was too late. She'd only taken an overnight bag to Zoe's. So she'd slipped out of Zoe's apartment before dawn and waited until Greyson left the house before she went inside, changed her clothes, and grabbed some supplies.

She'd stopped by the office next because she knew no one was there yet, but she'd learned her lesson. She didn't take the conservation's truck and ATV...she took Greyson's. His extra keys were at home, and he had his jeep.

She figured he owed her.

She'd gone to the same place where she and Greyson had seen the bald man, the man with the beard, and the foreign guy. She waited a while, but there were no sounds in the woods other than wild animals.

Hopping on Greyson's ATV, she drove further north. Whoever had been there before had changed their location. After what felt like forever, she heard engines up ahead. Quickly hiding Greyson's ATV, she ventured the rest of the way on foot.

Creeping up ahead, she crouched behind some boulders. She peeked over the top and saw a group of men with weapons standing together. They didn't look anything like the bald man and the man with the beard, and from what she could hear, they didn't have foreign accents. She quietly pulled her two-way radio out of her pack and was getting ready to signal Trent when she smelled gun powder and gasoline behind her.

She tried to turn around, but a strong arm snaked around her neck. She clutched at the camo covered arm and tried to claw it off her, but it only tightened. She coughed and struggled to breathe, trying to maneuver herself into a position to use a jiu-jitsu move to free herself, but the person countered, clearly knowing self-defense.

They dragged her, kicking every step of the way, over to the group of men.

"Who the hell is that, Boss?" one of the man asked.

"A nosy biologist," said a voice she recognized.

He released her and shoved her into the center of the circle.

She scrambled to her feet and whipped around to face her attacker in stunned disbelief. "Abe?"

"Sergeant Major to you." He smirked at her, and suddenly she didn't like him so much. She should have known he was ex-military with his salt and pepper flat top.

"I thought you were a hunter?"

"I *am* a hunter. I'm just hunting something different this time."

"Well, what do you want?"

"I want a lot of things, Sparrow. Hell, I deserve a lot of things. I *earned* them. Ever since I retired, they act like I don't exist anymore. Like I'm not important anymore." His face hardened into someone she didn't recognize. "Well, I'll show them."

"I'm sorry. I can only imagine how frustrating that must be for you." Maybe if she kept him talking, he would forget why he grabbed her, and she could find a way out. "If you let me go, I won't tell anyone what I saw."

"I wish I could believe you. I really do. I'm not an evil person. I like you, Sparrow, but you don't know how to keep your nose out of other people's business. I get it. I wanted to fight the whole world after my Anabelle passed, but I couldn't do that. I had a son who counted on me. I pulled myself together and worked hard, but my son grew up and the military forgot about me. Everyone abandoned me. I relied on family to pull me through, and I started over. Just like you're trying to do. You should have left well enough alone."

"What are you going to do with me?"

"You're a loose end, now. I can't have you interrupting the biggest business deal of my life. This will set me and my boy up for the rest of our lives."

A rider with a helmet on pulled up on an ATV.

"Perfect timing. Hey, son," he hollered. "Get on over here and take this trespasser to the shack."

The man took off his helmet.

Sparrow gasped. "Harlow?"

In all the time they'd been engaged, Harlow had never talked about his father, other than to say they were estranged. She'd never even seen a picture of the man. She opened her mouth to say something, but the look in Harlow's eyes stopped her. She'd seen that look of fear before. He barely shook his head no, but she saw it. Why didn't he want his father to know who she was?

Abe's gaze sliced to her and narrowed. "How do you know my son?"

She stiffened her spine. "I met him in town, same as you."

"Guess we both got a little careless this time. It won't happen again." His gaze hardened on Harlow. "I said take her to the shack, boy, and be quick about it. We have a meeting soon. I'm not about to let anything interrupt it this time."

Harlow nodded, then marched over to Sparrow and grabbed her arm, pulling her after him. He didn't stop walking until they reached the ATV. "Go along with what I do, please," he whispered.

Normally, she would put up a fight, but even after two years, she knew him. The look in his eyes said he wouldn't hurt her. She had nothing to lose and everything to gain by trusting him. He climbed on the ATV and shoved her over his lap, his hand gentling as it rested on her back.

Why was he putting on a show?

Gunning the engine, he drove off with her deep into the woods to a random shack and cut the engine. She scrambled off the ATV and he let her. He didn't even try to stop her from running. She started to run away, but then she came back.

"What are you doing?" he hissed. "You need to go."

"No," she said and crossed her arms.

"He'll send others if I'm gone too long."

"I need answers, and you owe me that much."

He let out a long breath. "I know. You have every right to hate me, especially after losing our baby."

Pain sliced through her over his words. "You knew about the baby?"

He was already shaking his head. "Not until I went to see Greyson in the hospital. He would have beat me up if he could. He told me all you've gone through. He's a good man. He loves you, you know."

She barked out a laugh. "If that's love, then I don't want it. He knew you were alive, but he didn't tell me, even after knowing all I had gone through. He knew about my sightings of you and thinking I was losing my mind, and he still didn't tell me."

"Because I told him not to."

"Why would he listen to you?" Harlow wasn't making any sense.

"You would have done anything to get answers about what had happened to me, right?"

She nodded.

"Well, Greyson would do the same for his mother."

"I don't get it."

"I know where she is, Sparrow. I made him promise to keep you out of the woods in exchange for that information. She's closer than you realize."

She felt her eyes bug. "Why would you do that?"

Harlow threw up his hands. "Because my father's a madman."

"Then why do you stay with him?"

"I'm all that he has left. First my mother died, but he pulled it together and raised me. He had a great career, but he spiraled out of control when he retired. Started acting crazy and demanding they take him back. When they didn't, he didn't know how to handle life. He wanted me to go to work with him. I told him I loved my career, and I told him I had a fiancée but I never gave him your name."

"You never told me anything about your father."

"And for good reason. I've never seen him so angry. He said I was his, and he would kill anyone who tried to take me away from him. I knew, if I chose you, he would kill us both. So when that bear attacked, it was the perfect opportunity to keep you safe. I needed to get him far away from you, so I convinced him we broke up and talked him into moving across the country to Coldwater Cove."

"I heard you mention The Cove before, so when you disappeared, I moved here to feel closer to you." Her face twisted with disgust. "Imagine my surprise when I found you here, still alive and well."

"I never thought you would come to Coldwater Cove. I tried to warn you away, but you wouldn't leave."

"You wrote the note?"

His brows drew together. "What note? I just meant showing up places, moving your things around, and making you think you were losing your mind, then having Greyson try to convince you to stay out of the woods. He told me the deal was off, and if I didn't tell you the truth, then he would."

"So that was why he met you by the woods."

"You saw us?" His eyes widened.

"Yes."

"Did you tell anyone?" A look of alarm flashed over his face.

"What did you do with Lily?"

"I don't know what you're talking about."

She shook her head. "I don't believe you."

ATVs sounded in the distance.

"Shit. I'll always love you, Sparrow, but I have to go for good this time. Run, and don't look back." He turned around, gunned his four-wheeler, and took off in the opposite direction until he disappeared from her vision.

Only, this time she wasn't sad.

Sparrow quickly looked in the shack. No Lily. She turned around and started running in the other direction. She ran as fast and as hard as she could and thought she was outwitting them when suddenly the sound of another ATV turned in her direction.

Oh, God, not again.

Pumping her legs, she cut through the trees towards the sound of the water. She didn't know if she had it in her to jump again. Not without Greyson. If only she had talked to him, she would have discovered the truth. And now she might die before ever getting to tell him that she loved him. If Abe found out Harlow had let her go, she had a feeling he wouldn't hesitate to kill her and kill his own son.

She no longer loved Harlow, but she didn't want to see him dead, either.

She scrambled over the last hill and skidded to a stop. An ATV was stopped between her and the river. She couldn't run anymore. She was exhausted. Dropping her pack, she took a defensive stance when it suddenly dawned on her.

That was Greyson's ATV and helmet she'd borrowed and hid in the woods.

The person flipped the visor on their helmet up, and familiar eyes stared back at her. The wild man, Mason Adler, was motioning for her to hop on. Using the last of her energy, she donned her pack and climbed onto the back of the ATV and held on tight.

* * *

"SPARROW!" Greyson ran over to meet his father as he pulled up to the crime scene.

Mason had been following Sparrow after he'd noticed her entering the woods. When he saw the men take her, he sent a message to Trent where the deal was going down, and then he took the hidden ATV to rescue Sparrow.

She slid off the ATV and flew into Greyson's arms.

He held her for a moment, not saying anything. She felt amazing in his arms, her heartbeat strong against his. He closed his eyes, still shaking at the thought of nearly losing her. "I'm so sorry I didn't tell you right away about Harlow, and I'm sorry I told him about the baby. It just sort of slipped out."

"It's okay." She leaned back and looked him in the eyes. "I know why you told him, and I know why you didn't tell me." She kissed him on the lips and then hugged him tighter. "I'm sorry I didn't let you explain. And I'm sorry I took your truck and ATV."

"I'm just glad my father got to you in time."

She pulled back again and looked beyond him. Abe and several men were on their knees with their hands behind their backs, handcuffed. A massive amount of firearms were on the ground in the center of them.

She lifted confused eyes to him. "Where's Harlow?"

"I was going to ask you that."

"Abe is his father."

Greyson gaped at her. "He is?"

"Yes. He ordered him to take me to the shack. I think that meant kill me. Harlow let me go and explained how his father was crazy, and everything he'd ever done was to protect me. Then he took off."

"Do you believe him?"

"I think I actually do." She looked around again. "But if he's not here, then where do you think he is?"

Greyson looked over at Abe. "Probably getting as far away from his father as possible."

"Let him go," she whispered.

His gaze met hers. "Yeah?"

"Yeah." She nodded.

"Do you still love him?" Greyson held his breath.

"I can honestly say no. The man I once knew died a couple years ago. I finally have the closure I was looking for."

"That makes one of us. With him gone, I guess I'll never know what happened to my mother."

"I'm so sorry. Maybe Abe knows." She looked at Trent, Hank, and… "Is that Ozzy Price and Peter LaCroix?"

"Yeah." Greyson scratched his head. "Special Agents Price and LaCroix are from the Federal Bureau of Alcohol, Tobacco, Firearms, and Explosives. Apparently, they've been undercover looking into weapons trafficking in this area for a while now. They've had their eye on these gun runners for a long time."

"I knew they weren't really biologists." Sparrow punched the air.

Greyson quirked a brow. "How so?"

"They didn't smell like a science lab. Even outdoors, some chemicals are unmistakable. At least on diehards like me."

He chuckled. "Better tell them that for future undercover work."

Sparrow's grin slipped. "Where's Lily?"

He sobered over the mention of Lily. "No one's talking, but they did spill the beans on not working alone."

"What do you mean? More people are involved?"

"I always wondered how they seemed to be one step ahead of us. They knew where our cameras were and what sections of the woods were safe to be in." Greyson shook his head, wondering how he had missed the signs. "My assistant, Willy, was tipping them off for a share of the profits."

"Oh, wow, that's terrible."

Greyson took a deep breath. "He wasn't the only one."

"Wait, there's more?"

"Tommy Flemming."

Sparrow sucked in a breath. "Oh, no, poor Laura."

"Abe approached him two years ago to help them

store guns in his warehouse and then smuggle them across state lines in the cars he moved on tractor trailers. Trent sent some deputies and Hank sent some officers to back each other up and go get Tommy for questioning."

"This is going to devastate Laura. She said he hasn't been happy since she became mayor. He's not in the spotlight anymore, and I don't think he can handle that."

Greyson frowned. "I just thought of something. What if Lily saw Tommy, and he took her. We've been looking in the woods the whole time. He could have easily hidden her in his warehouse."

"It's worth a shot. Let's go."

THE WHOLE TOWN was standing outside of Tommy Flemming's warehouse, watching the firefighters try to put out the flames. Trent, his deputies, Hank, and his officers were all there. When they'd arrived in town to bring Tommy in for questioning, the warehouse with all his cars stored inside was on fire.

"Tommy Flemming, you're under arrest," Trent said, feeling horrible for having to do this to Laura.

"Tommy, what's happening?" Laura wrapped her arms around her middle. "I don't understand."

"It'll be okay, Laura. This is all just a big misunderstanding." Tommy tried to hug her, but she stepped away by Stacy. He faced Trent with a desperate look in his eyes. "Buddy, I don't know what you're talking about. I'm not an arsonist."

"I'm not saying you are," Trent said carefully.

"Then what am I under arrest for?"

"Aiding and abetting gun runners for a cut of the profits," Hank said, having no problem walking forward and cuffing Tommy.

Tommy's eyes widened, and he quickly shot Sparrow a glare, then turned his gaze back to Hank. "You can't prove anything."

"You might not be an arsonist, but that doesn't mean you didn't have someone light your warehouse on fire for you." Trent frowned.

"Is that why you took out more insurance on the warehouse?" Laura asked. "You had all those business meetings for a bunch of new sales."

"Exactly. Business was booming, so I upped my insurance for my inventory. That makes perfect sense." Tommy looked at her pleadingly. "You have to believe me, babe."

"I don't have to do anything," she said. "You're not the man I married. You haven't been for a while now."

"That's because you think you're better than me. You're not. I was the star football player. Everyone loved me. The town used to look up to me, now all they see is you."

"Is that why you said yes to helping move the guns?" Greyson asked. "They already confessed and identified you. Willy, too. We know he was the lookout."

"A fire isn't enough to cover up all the evidence," Hank said. "Where's Lily?"

"I don't know what you're talking about," Tommy said, but his face was filled with fear as his eyes darted around as if looking for a way out.

"There's no getting out of this, Tommy, but right now your charges aren't a death sentence. Tell us what you know, and things will go better for you. If we find human bones in those ashes, you're looking at murder."

"Where's my wife?" Mason Adler took a step toward Tommy with his hands balled into fists.

Greyson put his hand on his father's shoulder until he looked at him. "You good?"

Mason relaxed his hands and looked at his son, then nodded. Without his helmet and having had a chance to get cleaned up, he looked like a completely different person. Short hair and clean shaven suited him. He looked like an older version of his son.

"You're all crazy. I want to talk to my lawyer," Tommy said, and then didn't speak again.

* * *

SPARROW SAT in the conservation truck, waiting on Victoria in her driveway. They were short staffed without Lily, so she'd offered to work with Sparrow. Chris was off finishing up the work in the woods at Sparrow and Lily's old site. Victoria hadn't been in the field in a while and had forgotten something for her pack, so they'd swung back for it.

Sparrow sat pondering over everything that had happened while her boss went in to get it. She was happy to be back with Greyson and things were better than ever, but so much had happened. His father had returned home, taking one of the upstairs bedrooms for now. He said he wanted Tia to find him a small place of his own on the outskirts of town, and they were looking at places that very day.

Meanwhile, Sparrow had gone back to work, and Greyson was still healing at home.

His father had finally accepted that he might never know what happened to his Carolyn, so it was time to rejoin the living. He wanted a relationship with his son, and Greyson was open to it, no matter how his grandparents felt about him. Mason was still his father. But he knew Greyson and Sparrow needed some time alone together. Besides, he'd said that cottage had always been Carolyn's dream.

Sparrow had her closure.

Abe and his men were in jail along with Tommy and Willy. No one had seen or heard from Harlow, but this time Sparrow wasn't sad. She felt free and at peace, as much as she could be. When the ashes cooled there were weapons found, but no human remains. Sparrow, Victoria, and Chris were devastated to think Lily was most likely lost to them forever, just like Greyson's mother, but they too realized life must go on.

She glanced at her watch. What was taking her boss so long? Hopping out of the truck, she went to knock on the door, but the door was open a crack.

She stepped inside. "Victoria? Do you need help? We need to get a move on. It's getting late." She walked farther inside, but no one was there. She saw a door to her bedroom in the back cracked open with a light on.

Walking into the room, she saw her boss lying on the floor, unconscious. Sparrow rushed to her side and felt for a pulse. Did she have a heart attack? Her pulse was beating, but blood was trickling from her head. Did she trip and hit her head?

"Hang on, Victoria. I've got you. You're going to be okay." Sparrow pulled her cellphone out and was about to dial 911 when a sharp pain shot through her head, and she fell unconscious on the floor.

What felt like hours later, Sparrow tried to open her eyes, but she had a blindfold on and a gag in her mouth. Her hands were tied behind her back, and she was on the hard floor. She moaned, and all of a sudden, someone grunted next to her.

She wasn't alone.

She grunted again, and the other person grunted in return. It sounded high pitched like a woman's voice. She started scooting in the direction of the voice until she bumped into someone. They both stilled. Scooting her back to the woman, she reached behind her and felt a long, thick braid and sighed in relief.

Lily.

Feeling for her hands, Sparrow gave a squeeze of reassurance and started to think. Where were they?

Who had them? And how would they escape? Too many questions warred in her head, so she decided to focus on her senses. In jiu-jitsu, she had learned how to home in on her other senses.

Moving away from Lily so she could try to pick up on the other smells in the room, she detected a lingering hint of bacon and seafood. The floor was cold, and the room smelled musty. Like someone's basement. She breathed deeply once more and paused.

She knew that smell.

A hint of chemicals. Not antiseptic like Nigel used. Something stronger. Like formaldehyde. She'd seen plenty of preserved animal parts during her college biology days. Pushing herself up the wall, she went on a hunch and started scooting her way along the wall. Not an easy task with her hands and feet tied.

She had traveled quite a ways, following the smell which was getting stronger. Finally, she came to a shelf. She couldn't lift her hands to reach it, but she pressed her cheek against it. Cool like glass, just as she'd thought. Glass was used for preserving wet specimens. Using her shoulder, she bumped the shelf over and over until one jar fell to the floor with a crash.

She dropped to the floor carefully and felt around with her fingers, avoiding the burning liquid as much as she could. She kept wincing in pain at cut after cut until she touched the edge of the jar. A big enough piece of glass to do the trick.

Using a sawing motion, she kept sawing at the duct tape around her wrists. Tears rolled down her face over the cuts to her flesh. It burned so badly, and the liquid was making her dizzy. She was trying not to inhale the toxic liquid.

Just as she felt faint, her hands broke free.

She scrambled away and pulled off the bandage around her eyes. Moving far away from the mess on the floor, she reached the wall and took a cleansing breath. She blinked. Lily sat on the floor with Victoria next to her.

Sparrow finished untying herself, and then got to work quickly on the other women.

"Sparrow," Lily cried. "I never thought I would see anyone again." She hugged her hard and then her eyes traveled to their boss. "What is Victoria doing here?"

"We were about to go into the field to do some work but had to stop at her place for something she forgot," Sparrow said.

"I went into my bedroom when someone hit me over the head," Victoria said.

"Did you see or hear anything?" Sparrow asked.

"No. I don't remember anything else. Where are we?" Victoria rubbed her head.

"I don't know," Lily said. "The person who took me never speaks. They just bring me food every morning and night and help me go to the bathroom. That's been it for weeks. I was losing my mind. Whoever it is has a chemical smell."

"Formaldehyde," Sparrow said.

"I knew it smelled familiar." Lily nodded.

Victoria took a couple steps toward the far side of the basement. "What's back there?" She shaded her eyes, trying to see.

"I took a hunch there were wet specimens back there, like we studied in school. I knocked one over." Sparrow showed her bloody wrists and fingers. "That's how I cut myself loose but be careful. The solution is strong. Inhaling too much of that would be lethal."

"There's something much bigger against that back wall." Victoria pointed. "See? What is that?"

"I don't know." Sparrow looked around. "There has to be a light switch around here." She walked over to the bottom of the stairs and sure enough, there was a light switch. She flicked it on, and the women screamed behind her.

Spinning around in a ready stance, she scanned the room for danger, then covered her mouth and gagged. There, in a life size glass container, was a perfectly preserved woman Sparrow recognized from photos she'd seen.

Greyson's mother, Carolyn Adler.

"Let's go," she said to the woman. "Whoever took us will be coming back soon. It's nearly dark outside. Follow me."

They ran up the stairs and tried the door. It was locked. Running back down the stairs, they looked for a window. This house was old, and the windows were small, not like the egress windows big enough for fireman in modern homes.

"I'm small," Sparrow said. "I can fit, but I can't reach it by myself."

"We'll lift you up," Victoria took charge. "Lily come over here and face me. I know you're tired from being tied up all this time, but we can't do this alone. I'm the tallest, so help Sparrow climb onto my shoulders, and I'll lift her up."

Sparrow shed all of her outer clothing right down to a simple t-shirt and tight jeans.

Lily did as Victoria instructed, and together they lifted Sparrow up. Even for her petite frame, this was going to be a tight fit, but she could do it. She had to. Wrenching the window open she pulled on it until it snapped off at the hinges. She threw it out of the way then blew out all her air and sucked in her stomach, pushing her way through the opening with their help.

Cold crisp air made her shiver, but she made it.

She rolled to her feet and said, "Hang tight. I'll go around the front and let you out." She turned around and ran to the front of the house but stopped short as a vehicle pulled into the driveway.

It couldn't be.

A man got out and walked toward her, puffing out his chest. "You really didn't think much of me when you first met me, did you, Sparrow?" He pushed his small spectacles up his nose.

"Chris Higgins?" She gaped at the short bald senior wildlife biologist.

"That's *Doctor* Higgins to you." He glanced around, but he lived on the outskirts of town. There were only a couple of houses nearby, but they were vacant.

"You're supposed to be in the field." She was stalling, still processing what was happening and what her next move would be.

"And you're supposed to be dead. Why won't you die already?" His eyes looked a little wild like he'd been smelling too much formaldehyde with his insane hobby. "You've ruined everything. My buyers backed out. No one will work with me anymore, not even the arms dealers. I counted on those referrals."

So that was how Harlow knew where Greyson's mother was.

Chris took a step towards her, looking bigger suddenly. "It's all your fault. I had a perfect little operation going. I find the species my clients are looking for and point them in the right direction, making sure no one is in those areas at the time. Until you came along and ventured into areas you weren't supposed to. Why won't you ever listen?" He took another step toward her.

"You're the one who was working with the poachers Zoe caught on the boat full of illegal animal parts and stolen live animals."

"That was just one of my clients. I'm important, you know. Victoria acts like I'm not. I earned that doctorate degree, and she won't even let me use it. And the pay is terrible for what we do. These people pay me well."

"They butcher animals for a single part, and they steal others to sell to illegal pet stores. You work for the department of conservation. You're supposed to help preserve animals, not destroy them."

"I do my part in preserving. Did you see my little collection?"

"I saw Carolyn Adler. You're a monster."

"She was already dead. The people I work with tried to get Mason to teach them survival skills and help them navigate the woods. He refused, so they took his wife to blackmail him. They didn't count on her being a fighter. She attacked one of my clients, and he killed her. I don't do the killing, but I was fascinated with trying to preserve a full human being. She turned out well, don't you think?" He was serious, his crazy eyes filling with pride. The man was delusional.

"Your little operation is over now," Sparrow said, confident she could take him in a fight.

"It's not little!" he roared and pulled out a gun.

She froze. "You won't get away with this. People will hear a gunshot."

"Those houses are for sale. Like you said. Everyone thinks I'm in the field. They think you and Victoria are in the field as well. And they've written Lily off. Maine woods are harsh. Tragic things happen."

He cocked the hammer and pointed the barrel at her head just as she dropped low and used her shinbone to kick his legs, knocking him off his feet. It was powerful and she didn't have to take her eyes off her attacker like with a spinning kick. He went flying backward, with his feet flipping out from beneath him as his gun went off up in the air.

Wasting no time, she scrambled over to him and punched him when he tried to fight her. She flipped him over, pulled off her sock, and tied his wrists together.

A car pulled up seconds later. Tia got out of the driver's side and Mason jumped out of the passenger side. "We were looking at a house over here and heard the gunshot," she said. "What on earth happened?"

"Call 911," Sparrow said.

"Is anyone else in there?" Mason headed for the door.

"Stay here and watch him, Mason," Sparrow quickly said. "I'll get the girls." She couldn't let him see his wife. That would destroy him. She owed him that much for saving her in the past. "And Mason?"

"Yeah?" He looked up at her from the ground as he knelt by Chris.

"Call your son. You're going to need each other." Then she disappeared before the sad knowing filling Mason's eyes with unshed tears destroyed her.

In such a short time, he'd become as important to her as Greyson, and she'd need to stay strong to help them through the horrible grief to come. Everyone in Coldwater Cove was like family. Sparrow had no doubts her newfound friends would rally to help heal this family...

Her family.

EPILOGUE

SPARROW SAT beside Greyson on the patio of their home one year later, enjoying the fall weather and some peace and quiet. Mason sat in a chair beneath Carolyn's favorite tree at the cottage, down by the ocean, rocking his new granddaughter, Carolyn Adler, who they called Lynie.

After they'd arrested Chris and freed Victoria and Lily, they had finally laid Carolyn to rest properly right there beneath her favorite tree. Mason had decided not to move. Living at the cottage wasn't so bad after all, but he'd had a small cabin built on the property further down by the ocean, by his love.

The three of them had become a family.

Greyson had asked Sparrow to marry him, not wanting to waste any more time, and Sparrow had agreed. They'd had a whirlwind wedding, much to his grandparents' and her parents' dismay.

But they were quickly forgiven after conceiving a honeymoon baby.

His grandparents were coming around a lot more often, even making peace with Mason. And her parents, brother, and sister were planning a trip to see the baby soon. Her family was finally whole.

"I love our life," Sparrow finally said.

"I love *you*." Greyson kissed her hand. "Hey, isn't Laura due back with the twins soon?"

"Yes, in two weeks. She told Stacy this leave of absence with the kids was the best decision she's made in a long time. They've really enjoyed their time on the West Coast with her family."

"That's great." Greyson nodded. "The whole town has been worried about her and wondering if she'd even come back. Councilman Johnson has done a good job while she's been gone."

"He sure has, considering she left some pretty big shoes to fill." Sparrow's smile waned a little.

Greyson squeezed her hand. "What's going on in that pretty little head of yours?"

"Do you think she'll stay? What if she comes back and gives her resignation?"

"That's up to Laura, sweetheart, but I get what you're saying. She's been the backbone of this town ever since she set out to fill Elizabeth Buchannan's shoes and clean up The Cove. I can't imagine this place without her."

"Me neither." Sparrow remained quiet for a moment, then perked up with good news to share. "On a happier note," she said, her smile returning as she shifted in her chair to face the man she'd love forever, "Jack finally asked Zoe to marry him. Emma and Gunner are here for the engagement party and for Olivia and Hank's wedding."

"It's about time Jack proposed. I'm glad his sister and her fiancé are back. Jack needs all the guidance he can get." Greyson laughed. "He never officially asked Zoe to move in, she just never renewed her lease."

"Well, that's Zoe for you. She was too stubborn to tell him what she wanted, so she simply made it happen. Obviously, he didn't mind. I'm just glad he proposed because Lord only knew what she would have done to make that happen." Sparrow smiled.

She had the best friends she could ever imagine, and they were right there for her from the very beginning. The Cove gave people exactly what they needed whether they realized it or not. She had needed to love again and to start a family, and Greyson had given her that.

"Speaking of things that took forever, can you believe Buck and Tia have been together for a year now?" He shook his head in wonder.

"That's only because Tia told him if he didn't step up his game, she was out." Sparrow laughed, thinking of the spunky realtor's assertiveness.

"Well, that's one way to get what you want." Greyson joined in her laughter, and the gleam of sheer happiness in his eyes had her counting her blessings.

"I never knew what I wanted before, but I do now." Their connection was like nothing she'd ever experienced. She felt her body tingle to life just being near him, and her mind moved to more delectable thoughts as she gazed once more at their daughter in the loving arms of her grandfather. They had a few more hours of freedom before the baby would need to be fed.

"Yeah?" He looked down at her as if he could read her mind and stared hungrily at her lips.

"Yeah." She licked hers in anticipation. A thrill zipped through her body when his eyes clouded with building passion. "A house full of children. I want a big family, Grey."

"And I want you." He leaned down and kissed her softly. "When you're ready."

"Oh, I'm ready now." And she didn't want to waste another second.

"But Lynie is only two months old. Are you sure you're up to it?"

"I got the all-clear two weeks ago from my doctor." Her smile came slow and sweet. "Come with me, my husband. The Cove isn't the only thing that will give you what you need."

"Now, how can I say no that?"

ABOUT THE AUTHOR

Kari Lee Townsend is a National Bestselling Author of mysteries & a tween superhero series. She also writes romance and women's fiction as Kari Lee Harmon. With a background in English education, she's now a full-time writer, wife to her own superhero, mom of 3 sons, 1 darling diva, 1 daughter-in-law & 2 lovable fur babies. These days you'll find her walking her dogs or hard at work on her next story, living a blessed life.

Naughty or Nice (Merry Scroog-mas novella #1)

Brook (Lakehouse Treasures novella #4)
Meghan (Lakehouse Treasure novella #3)
Amber (Lakehouse Treasures novella #2)
James (Lakehouse Treasures novella #1)

Sleeping in the Middle (Comfort Club #1)

Love Lessons
Project Produce

Spurred by Fate (Triple R Ranch short story #2)
Destiny Wears Spurs (Triple R Ranch #1)

Frozen Waters (Coldwater Cove #2)
Dark Seas (Coldwater Cove #1)

Valley of Secrets
Until Tomorrow

Jingle all the Way (Merry Scroog-mas novella #3)
Sleigh Bells Ring (Merry Scroog-mas novella #2)
Naughty or Nice (Merry Scroog-mas novella #1)

Brook (Lakehouse Treasures novella #4)
Meghan (Lakehouse Treasure novella #3)
Amber (Lakehouse Treasures novella #2)
James (Lakehouse Treasures novella #1)

Sleeping in the Middle (Comfort Club #1)

Love Lessons
Project Produce

Spurred by Fate (Triple R Ranch short story #2)
Destiny Wears Spurs (Triple R Ranch #1)